LOST IN THE BAYOU

Lightning flashed overhead when the two men pushed through the underbrush and came upon a narrow path that lead deeper into the swamp. Warren pointed, his finger stabbing in the direction the path led. "He had to go that way. If he went straight, he'd end up bogged down in the bayou. He had to take that path!"

Before Chance could suggest that they both return to the house, Warren was running. With a curse, the gambler followed him. A half-mile later, Chance stumbled to a halt. The young man wasn't there. Nor could Chance find any trace of him.

"Warren! Warren!" Chance shouted.

But only the pounding rain and thunder answered him . . .

CHANCE

#9

DEADLY DEAL

CLAY TANNER

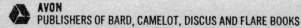

AVON
PUBLISHERS OF BARD, CAMELOT, DISCUS AND FLARE BOOKS

CHANCE #9: DEADLY DEAL is an original publication of Avon Books.
This work has never before appeared in book form.

AVON BOOKS
A division of
The Hearst Corporation
105 Madison Avenue
New York, New York 10016

Copyright © 1988 by George W. Proctor
Published by arrangement with the author
Library of Congress Catalog Card Number: 87-91697
ISBN: 0-380-75433-9

First Avon Books Printing: January 1988

AVON TRADEMARK REG. U.S. PAT. OFF. AND IN OTHER COUNTRIES, MARCA
REGISTRADA, HECHO EN U.S.A.

Printed in the U.S.A.

K-R 10 9 8 7 6 5 4 3 2 1

This one is for Al Sarrantonio,
a fellow stargazer and wordsmith

ONE

The young woman disappeared!

Chance Sharpe bolted straight up on the taxi's leather seat. His head snapped around in a classic double take. One moment the attractive brunette had walked along the St. Louis streets with an eager terrier straining on the end of a long leash. In the blinking of an eye, both woman and dog vanished!

The riverboat gambler shifted a long, slender saber cigar from one side of his mouth to the other. His cool, steel blue eyes surveyed the street beyond the cab's window. He saw nothing, except for a sparse sprinkling of men who hastened through the early morning with collars high and hands clutching stovepipe hats securely atop their heads against a whistling December wind. Whether the men's brisk strides carried them toward waiting jobs or returned them from an overstayed visit with the night's pleasures, Chance could only guess.

Exhaling a gust of blue tobacco smoke, the gambler shook his head while he continued to scan the street. He would have wagered a hefty bundle that the alluring brunette had been real and not some tantalizing fragment of a most pleasant dream.

And I would have lost, he admitted to himself. A woman—or a man—simply did not evaporate from a street in the space of a single stride. The night had

been long and tiring. The taxi's rhythmic sway had
been all that was needed to lull him into a gentle sleep.
A touch of chagrin moved across his lips; he had nodded off for an instant without even knowing it. Another moment might have deposited the cigar clenched
between his teeth into the lap of the expensive bur-
gundy-hued suit he wore. *That would have been a rude
and costly awakening!*

Chance refused to concede a harsher mental reprimand. The night had been too good to him for self-
recriminations. The weight of the thousand dollars
stuffed into a wallet inside his coat was proof of that.
A private poker game, lasting from evening to dawn,
had proved to be a battle of wits as well as luck with
some of St. Louis's most prominent businessmen. He
had lost as many hands as he had won, the difference
being that he bet only on those he won. The long night
doubled his original five-hundred-dollar stake—a sum
that most men struggled years to earn in the postwar
United States.

An excited, high-pitched yapping pulled the gambler
from his satisfied reflections. A brown and white terrier darted from a dark alley. A leather leash minus the
attractive brunette who had once held it trailed from
the animal's neck, whipping over the ground like an
agitated snake.

She wasn't a dream! Adrenaline coursed through the
riverboat gambler's veins; his temples pounded. Something was wrong, very wrong! "Driver," Chance
shouted, "stop the cab!"

The dappled gray drawing the hack slowed its pace
as the driver hauled back on the reins and called out,
"Whoa there, Sarah."

Chance didn't wait for the cab to roll to a halt.
Throwing open the carriage door, he sprang to the
street and ran toward the alley the terrier had fled. The

wind's whistle could not disguise the scrambling shuffle of feet and the muffled feminine cries of distress that came from within. The gambler's right hand slipped beneath his coat, found a fobbed, gold watch chain dangling from a vest pocket. One smart tug brought a double-barreled .22-caliber Wesson derringer from the pocket into his palm.

The worst of his suspicions were realized when he darted into the shadowed alley. Not one, but two ruffians held the brunette pinned between them against a brick wall. The larger of the two, a gorilla of a man with a shaven scalp and a six-foot height that equaled the gambler's, clamped a rough paw over the woman's mouth to silence her.

"She's a pretty one, ain't she, Bigelow?" This from the shorter of the two, a black-haired man wearing a soiled stocking cap. "Too pretty just to slit her throat before we have our fun, wouldn't you say?"

A throaty sound that was a evil mockery of a decent man's laugh pushed from Bigelow's throat, and the massive man's face split in a wicked grin that displayed several missing teeth. "Ain't no reason why we can't have her 'fore we kill her, Chester. Ain't no reason at all!"

"My thoughts exactly." The smaller man reached to his belt and pulled free a knife with a wide, curved blade.

The young woman's eyes grew round with terror as he lifted the knife and held it before her face. Her body strained and twisted to no avail; the two men pressed their weight closer, holding her firmly against the cold brick.

Chester chuckled, obviously enjoying her struggle. "Ain't had a woman that didn't smell of onions since I can't remember. Can't think of a better way to start a new day. Strip her clothes off, Bigelow. I want this 'un as naked as the day she was born.''

Another evil chuckle rose from the shaven-headed gorilla's throat as his left hand lifted to the neck of his captive's coat. Before his meaty fingers dipped beneath the fabric and ripped downward, the distinctive metallic clinking of cocking hammers sounded through the empty alley.

"Unless you plan to begin and *end* this day with a breakfast of lead, I'd suggest that you release her." Chance's words met the men's cold stares when their gazes rolled to him. "And I'd be quick about it. My trigger finger gets a strange twitch in it this early in the morning."

A feral snarl stretched across Bigelow's face as his pawlike hands dropped from the woman. The smaller man, the one called Chester, half turned to the gambler but kept his hold on the brunette.

"I was addressing both of you when I spoke." Chance's right arm edged slightly to the left. The Wesson's twin barrels homed on a spot directly between Chester's eyes to emphasize his words. "Let her go—now!"

A low rumble worked its way up Bigelow's throat as his knife-wielding companion released the woman and spun to fully face the unexpected intruder. That sound burst from the shaven-scalp man's lips as a bestial roar. In a single heartbeat, Bigelow's right arm slashed up. Solidly the back of his hand smashed into the brunette's delicate chin. Her head snapped back to slam into unyielding brick. A piteous whimper escaped her trembling lips as she crumpled to the ground, dazed.

Simultaneously Bigelow pivoted on his left foot and launched himself toward Chance, who stood ten feet away.

Without flinching, the gambler swung the derringer back to the larger of the two cutthroats. Bigelow took one lunging stride, and Chance's forefinger squeezed around the unguarded triggers. Both barrels of the palm gun spat fire and lead.

A dark—deep purple, rather than scarlet—ragged hole opened in the center of Bigelow's forehead. The two slugs' impact jerked back the shaven head as though it had been struck by an invisible sledgehammer. An instant later, Bigelow's hulking body followed. He tumbled to the ground like a fallen oak, then lay there twitching spasmodically as death claimed him.

Chance's attention, however, homed on Chester, who leaped over the body of his fallen companion to lash out with the curved blade clutched in his right hand. Tossing aside the spent derringer, the gambler backstepped—not quickly enough. Like the kiss of a razor, the broad knife nicked a knuckle on the back of his left hand.

"That's but a sample of what's in store for you!" Chester's dark eyes glowed with decided relish as he lashed out once again. "First I'll open your gullet, then I'll have the pretty one there for myself."

Chance hastened, backstepping to avoid a high slash of the curved knife meant to slice his throat from ear to ear. His right hand once more shot beneath his coat. This time it found the handle of a belly-gun tucked beneath the waistband of his trousers. His thumb had cocked the .44-caliber Colt's hammer by the time he freed the pistol.

A brief instant of horrible recognition paled Chester's face when he saw the revolver. In the next moment, death exploded from the pistol's one-inch sawed-off barrel. Fingers desperately clawing at his chest as though to tear burning lead from his heart, the small man collapsed atop Bigelow's now still body—and died.

In a wide-legged stance, Chance stood over the two as if he expected them to rise. When they didn't, he moved across the alley and knelt beside the woman. "Are you all right?"

"Far better than I would have been if you hadn't happened along." Brown eyes flicked with specks of gold lifted to the gambler. A hint of a smile played at the corners of her mouth in spite of the fear that still strained her delicate features. "Are they dead?"

Chance ignored her question and handed her a handkerchief. "Here, use this. You have blood on your lower lip."

Without blanching, she daintily dabbed a corner of the silk at her mouth and shook her head. "I'm afraid that I bit the inside of my cheek when he struck me. Nothing serious." She glanced at him again, holding out a hand.

The gambler took her gloved fingers and helped her to her feet. Her head turned to the two dead assailants. "They are dead, aren't they?" Her tone was more statement than question.

"They left me with little choice." Chance shrugged, then stooped to retrieve his discarded derringer. He tucked the weapon back into his vest.

"You appear to need this handkerchief as much as I." A strand of dark brown hair tumbled across her forehead as she nodded at his left hand. "You're bleeding."

Chance glanced at the minor cut. "It's nothing. The little one nicked me with . . ."

The gambler's voice trailed away as his eyes found the offending blade on the ground near Chester's feet. A puzzled expression furrowed his brow when he bent to retrieve the knife. Perplexed, he turned the broad, curved blade over, closely examining it. "It's made of wood. I don't think that I've ever seen anything like this. Have you?"

"I'm afraid that my acquaintance with knives is limited to the utensils required for dining," she answered, once more glancing at the two dead men. "Shouldn't we inform the police or someone about what occurred here?"

The gambler nodded, took her arm, and began to lead her from the alley. "I'll do that as soon as I take you someplace safe. My hotel is two blocks away. We can wait in the lobby for the authorities."

Forced composure edged aside the fear in her expression as she nodded. "Agreed, as long as you let me take a look at that hand, Mr.—"

"Sharpe, Chance Sharpe," he answered, then added, "But there's no need to concern yourself with my hand. It's merely a nick, really."

"Nick or not," she insisted, "it's bleeding, and I want to look at it."

The gambler acquiesced with a gentle smile and . . .

His arm wouldn't move! He stumbled to an unsteady halt. Try as he did, the muscles in his left arm refused to respond to his mental commands. Like so much dead meat, his arm dangled at his side.

"What's wrong?" Fear once more invaded her gold-flecked eyes. "Is there something wrong?"

"I don't know." Chance shook his head with uncertainty. "My arm has gone cold and numb. It won't move."

Her gloved hands reached out and took his arm. "Come. We'll summon a physician when we reach the hotel."

The gambler didn't argue. The icy cold seeped from his arm into his chest, spreading through his body. He tried to follow the tug of her urgent hands, but couldn't. His legs had turned to immovable granite.

''I can't wa—''

Chance never finished the sentence. The cold rushed up like a tidal wave that broke within his head. The world around him whirled with ever-increasing madness. He tried to blink, to fight through the topsy-turvy spinning. His eyelids closed, but would not open. Like a soul separated from its body, he felt himself falling, tumbling into the inky blackness of a maelstrom that suddenly surrounded him.

Then there was nothing—except the freezing cold.

TWO

Through the icy cold that clenched each muscle of Chance Sharpe's body in an unbreakable grip, above the smothering blackness that blanketed the gambler's eyes from the light of day, he heard voices. Foremost came a deep, resonant voice weighted with ponderous pauses and syllables drawn out for interminable eternities.

At least, he thought, the sounds reaching his ears were strings of syllables. In truth he wasn't certain, since he was unable to distinguish a single word amid the tones that taunted his ears. Although he fought to deny the possibility, he could not avoid the reality that the incoherent noises were nothing more than delusions, hallucinations of a fever-ridden brain.

To accept the voices as mere deceptions of the mind would have been to cast aside the second voice—the dulcet tones of a woman. A background to the throaty male voice, the woman's syllables, garbled as they were, brimmed with concern and gentle caring. He could feel the shape of her voice delving through the blackness to reach him.

There were other sounds, other voices that resounded in his ears, but they were no more than distractions that muffled and muddled the woman's voice. He cursed their intrusion, voicelessly crying out for the return of those soothing feminine tones.

More real than the voices were the hands. He felt fingers and palms touching his body, shifting his weight. And there were the needlelike pricks! Again and again tiny daggers of pain bit into his fingertips and the soles of his feet, occasionally stinging at his arms and legs. Like a drunkard unable to sort through the blurred sensations deluging his brain, he could not comprehend those probing hands, the needles, nor the crushing pressure that slammed atop his chest time and again.

Both the voices and the hands came in snatches sandwiched between indeterminable periods of nothingness—time that he realized that he had drifted into unconsciousness.

He had no idea how long he faded in and out of those meaningless depths, nor did he care. Except for the voices and the hands, the periods of consciousness—no more than floating adrift between awaking and sleep—differed little from the oblivion of the blackness.

The spot of warmth at the center of his chest brought the first hint of change that he could differentiate as reality rather than dream. That heated glow gradually spread through his torso. The ice that locked his arms and legs melted before its tingling flow. His fingers and toes twitched—no longer cold granite, but living flesh once again. A voice lost to him in the darkness was reborn in a rasping groan. His head rolled from side to side atop the caressing softness of a down pillow.

Like veiling curtains pushed back to allow the morning to flood a dark room, his eyes opened. Light, bright beyond belief, stabbed at his eyes. He groaned again, twisting his head away from the painful brightness. He sucked in a breath to bolster his courage and pushed his eyelids wide once more. Relentless in its assault, the light rushed in with blinding brightness. He blinked and moaned, but the light refused to dim.

A blur moved over him, shielding his throbbing eyes from the actinic glare. He blinked again in an attempt to focus on the amorphous, shifting form. The image remained fuzzy and distorted. It didn't matter; the woman's soothing voice spoke, and this time he understood her words:

"Mr. Sharpe! You're awake! My God, you're awake!"

"Chance," he mumbled over a dry tongue whose tip seemed to be glued to the roof of his mouth. He pursed his lips and sucked. Enough saliva seeped over his tongue to loosen it. He attempted to speak a second time. "Chance . . . my father was Mr. Sharpe."

"Wait here, Mr. Shar—Chance. I'll be right back in a few minutes."

The joy and relief in the woman's tone brought a smile to the corners of his lips. Her reaction matched his own—he was alive! "I'm not going anywhere. I'll be right here."

The blur darted away, and the light returned. The rough edges of its harshness had been buffed away, but the brightness still jabbed at his eyeballs like a myriad of tiny needles. Blinking didn't ease the pain, nor did it bring the images about him into focus. He could feel that he lay flat on his back in a bed, but where he could only guess. The walls and the ceiling of the room around him were a mishmash of mismatched colors and shapes that ran grotesquely into one another.

My hotel room, he finally decided. His nose rather than his eyes led him to that conclusion. None of the smells he associated with a hospital invaded his nostrils. The coy scent of the woman's perfume lingered in the air. He silently approved of the musky fragrance with another smile.

Closing his eyes, he sighed. The blurred vision and the stabbing brightness of the light didn't matter. He was alive, and that was enough.

Dr. Kenneth Craighead lifted his head from Chance's bare chest, where he had listened to the gambler's heart for several minutes. "Your heart sounds strong enough—ticking like a Swiss watch." He looked at his patient and smiled.

Or it seemed to be a smile; Chance wasn't sure. His vision remained blurred, as though he viewed the world through a pond of rippling water. Dr. Craighead's snow white hair and beard were distinguishable, but his features were no more than a watery patch of pink amid all that stark white.

"And that, my friend, is a mite more encouraging than it sounded yesterday," the physician continued. "You stopped breathing six times during the morning and afternoon. We had to throw you over that beer barrel over there and roll you back and forth just like you were a man who had gone under for the third time."

Chance glanced across the hotel bedroom to barely make out the form of a wooden barrel on its side near the door. He now understood the pressure he had felt on his chest. "How long was I out?"

"Two days." Craighead ordered him to lift his right arm and then his left. He then repeated the process with his legs. "You seem to be functioning all right. How do you feel?"

"Weak." Chance squeezed and flexed both his hands. Neither had the strength to wring out a wet sponge.

"Not surprising. You're lucky to be alive," the physician answered. "You have Miss Walsh to thank for having the presence of mind to hail a cab, get you to the hotel, and then summon me. If she hadn't, you'd be six foot under right now. Not only did she save your life, but she's proved to be a capable nurse for these past two days."

"It is I who should be thanking Mr. Sharpe." The young woman glanced over the doctor's shoulder and smiled. "He saved me from death . . . and worse."

The woman was the same that Chance had rescued from Chester and Bigelow in the alley—at least, he thought she was. He couldn't discern her face through the shifting mist that distorted his vision. However, she had brunette hair, and her voice was that of the woman in the alley—the same voice that had spoken to him in the darkness.

"Miss Walsh . . ." The gambler started to thank her.

She waved him away. "Anne."

"Only if you drop the 'Mr. Sharpe,' " he answered.

"All right, Chance." She nodded and smiled again.

"What about your vision?" Dr. Craighead interrupted the exchange. "Is it improving?"

"Slowly," the gambler replied. "Everything's still watery and out of focus."

"That it's improving is a good sign. It will probably return to normal with time," the physician said. "And your strength will come back as soon as you get some food in your stomach. Two days without a decent meal is enough to leave most men feeling weak."

"*Probably* return to normal?" Chance arched a questioning eyebrow.

Craighead shrugged. "That's my guess."

"What do you mean *guess?*" the gambler pressed.

"It's hard to do anything but make an educated guess." The doctor shook his head. "I've never been around many poisoned men."

"Poisoned?" In spite of his weakness Chance pushed up on his elbows and stared at the physician.

Anne Walsh said: "It was on the knife that cut your hand. It was meant for me."

"You're lucky you received no more than a scratch," Craighead said. "In my estimation, it's one of the major reasons you're still alive. Enough of the poison didn't get into your system to kill you immediately."

Chance sank back, remembering the curved wooden knife that had nicked a knuckle on his left hand. *Poison?* He found it hard to accept. Poisoned blades were something only encountered in Shakespeare's plays. Even in New Orleans's French Quarter, poison was unheard of. Why use poison when a bullet or a knife drawn across a throat would suffice—and was quicker?

"Hot food—especially red meat—and rest are what you need now," Craighead said as he rose from the side of the gambler's bed and closed a black case. "I'll check back on you this evening. But unless I miss my guess, you'll be back to normal in two days."

Chance accepted the pronouncement without a protest. His riverboat the *Wild Card* wasn't due to dock at the St. Louis wharves for three more days. Weak or not, he fully intended to board that majestic lady of the river. He had been too long from her decks.

"See that he eats everything that I've ordered," the doctor directed Anne Walsh as he opened the hotel room's door. "I'll select a dinner for our patient when I return this evening."

Before the physician could exit, a short man wearing a brown pin-striped suit, with a derby sitting atop his head, pushed across the threshold and into the room. The man chewed a smoking stogie from one side of his mouth to the other as his slightly bulging eyes darted about the room, finally alighting on Chance. He then glanced at the physician. "I thought you were going to inform me the moment he came around."

Policeman, Chance identified the unannounced visitor. The man looked police, dressed police, and even his cheap smoke—probably of the two-for-a-nickel variety—smelled of police.

"Mr. Sharpe regained consciousness a few minutes ago," Craighead answered. "I've just completed his physical examination and was on my way to your office, Mr. Marshal."

"Detective Marshal," the man corrected, confirming the gambler's suspicion. "Is he up to a little talk?"

Craighead glanced at Chance, then nodded to the detective. "If it isn't too long. Mr. Sharpe needs his rest right now. He's still a weak man."

"Yeah, yeah." The policeman brushed the physician away with those two unconcerned utterances and walked to the gambler's bed. He stared down at Chance for several silent moments, then looked at Anne Walsh. "I'm going to have to ask you to leave the room."

Anne's lips parted as though to object, but she swallowed her words, nodded meekly, rose, and followed Dr. Craighead from the hotel room.

As the door closed, Detective Marshal's bulging eyes shifted back to Chance. "All right, friend, you've got a few questions to answer about those two men you killed, or else you'll be doing your recovering in a jail cell waiting for a hangman."

THREE

"Let's begin with why you went after those two men."
With each word he spoke, a scrawny mustache crawled
across Detective Marshal's upper lip like a malnour-
ished caterpillar.

Chance's steel blue eyes narrowed. When the policeman had entered the hotel room, he hadn't seen the
mustache; now it was clearly discernible. Unless Marshal's facial hair had sprouted magically in the past few
seconds, his vision was clearing. He moaned inwardly.
Why couldn't his eyes have focused on Anne Walsh's
pleasing visage?

"It won't do you no good to go tight-lipped,
Sharpe." A less than subtle undertone of menace
slipped into the detective's voice. "I came for information, and I intend to get it."

There were two ways to handle Detective Marshal's
heavy-handed approach—returning his boorishness in
kind or answering the man's questions and be rid of
him. While it might have been interesting to lock horns
with the rude officer on another occasion, Chance was
too weak and tired to be bothered with the man. All
he wanted was to see Marshal walk out of the hotel
room and never return. The most direct route to that
goal was answering the policeman's questions.

"I'll answer any questions you have, as soon as I
see some proper identification," the gambler said,

16

lacking the strength to hone the tenor of his voice with the cool edge he wanted.

The detective grunted, reached into his coat, and produced a silvered badge that identified him as Colbert Marshal. ''Now tell me what you were doing in that alley with Chester Ludd and Morris Bigelow.''

Beginning with his night-long poker game, Chance recounted the events that led to the attack in the alley and the shooting. Marshal listened, stopping the gambler here and there to request that he elaborate on his own background. Chance told the detective of his recent return from the Dakota Territory, and that he now waited for his sidewheeler the *Wild Card* to journey upriver before he traveled to New Orleans. Although he carefully avoided mentioning the reason for his overly long stay in Dakota—he had been accused of robbing a bank and murdering a teller in the process. There was no need to add fuel to the detective's suspicions.

Drawing a chair beside the bed, Marshal settled into the cushions while he asked the gambler to repeat the alleyway encounter—three times. By the time Chance concluded the third recitation of the incident, the detective's voice had returned to a civil tone.

''I think that just about covers everything I need, Mr. Sharpe.'' Marshal pushed the derby to the back of his head and chewed on his cigar a moment. ''Everything you've said checks with Miss Walsh's and the cabbie's stories. The thing that's still got me puzzled is why Ludd and Bigelow went after the girl in the first place.''

Marshal's abrupt change in tactics surprised the gambler. It was as though the detective sought his opinion. ''You'll have to ask Miss Walsh about that.''

''Already did. She claims never to have seen them before.'' The policeman sucked at his teeth and shook his head. "Ludd and Bigelow were nothing but lowlife drifters. You probably did the world a favor back in the alley. They damned sure won't be missed. Each had a record of petty crimes as long as my arm, but murder was out of their league. It just doesn't make sense for them to go after the girl—especially with this."

Marshal reached into his coat again to pull out the wooden blade that Chester Ludd had wielded. The detective turned it over on his palm. "Never seen anything that comes close to this before. And Doc Craighead can't identify the poison that was on it. You ever seen one like this or even similar?"

Chance accepted the thin wooden weapon, making certain not to nick himself on the razor-honed blade. One bout with its deadly poison was enough. He doubted that he would survive a second.

"No need to worry about the blade. Doc got all the poison off. I made doubly sure by testing it out on an alley mongrel yesterday. It's safe." An amused smile played across Marshal's lips as he watched the gambler.

Chance still kept his fingertips away from the sharp edge. After studying the knife's skilled workmanship, he shook his head. "To be honest, I can't even identify the wood used to carve this."

"Wood don't matter. I'm more interested in the poison." Marshal held up his hands when the gambler tried to return the knife. "Keep it as a souvenir—a reminder of how lucky you are to still be breathing."

Chance placed the wooden blade on a table beside the bed and watched Detective Marshal rise. Halfway to the door, the policeman turned and looked back at the gambler. "You got an address in New Orleans, in case I have to get in touch with you later?"

"The Hotel Burgundy," Chance replied. "Or you can wire my attorney, Philip Duwayne."

Marshal took a small notebook from a coat pocket and scribbled in it with a pencil. Without another word or parting gesture, he turned and opened the room's door. As he left, Anne Walsh entered, carrying a covered silver tray. The enticing aroma of roast beef wafted in the gambler's nostrils.

Adjusting the pillows to support his back, he sat straight in bed. "If it tastes half as good as it smells, it will be a banquet!"

"Prime rib cooked medium-rare with baked potato and coffee." Anne placed the tray across Chance's lap, lifted its silver cover, and beamed down at him. "Dr. Craighead ordered this, and left instructions that you were to eat every bite. He said that you were to rest again then, and *if* you felt up to it, you could take your evening meal in the hotel's dining room this evening."

The gambler wasn't thinking about dinner; the minor feast spread before him was all the food he wanted to consider for the moment. Lifting knife and fork, he attacked the rare meat with a vengeance. Half the prime rib was neatly disposed of before he came up for air.

"You *are* hungry, aren't you?" Anne arched a pleasingly shaped eyebrow in amusement while she settled into the chair that Detective Colbert Marshal had left beside the bed.

"Like a wolf!" Chance's gaze traced over the delicate features of the young brunette's face before his attention returned to the bountiful meal and the as-of-yet-untouched baked potato. "I feel as though I haven't eaten in at least a week or five."

Anne's laughter chimed, and the flecks of gold in her brown eyes came alive with an interior light that flashed like miniature gems. "It's good to see that you have such a healthy appetite. After Dr. Craighead told me why you collapsed in the alley, I was frightened that you might never breathe again, let alone eat.''

''If I'd been in the position to be afraid, I would have been, too,'' the gambler assured her with an understanding smile between alternating bites of beef and potato. ''I'm just glad I didn't know what had happened until it was over.''

While Chance continued to work on his meal, Anne spoke of herself and her family. ''This is our first visit to Saint Louis since the war ended—at least, it is for my mother and my younger brother, Warren. My father's traveled upriver several times on business. James and Elouise came with him last fall.''

''Then you're not from Saint Louis?'' Chance hastily washed down a mouthful of beef with a sip of hot black coffee.

''No.'' Anne shook her head, setting the long curls of her deep nut brown hair astir. ''We have a plantation just outside New Orleans. My father purchased it a few years before the war broke out.''

Chance nodded. The Walsh family was damned lucky to still have its land. More families than the gambler wanted to count had lost their farms and plantations in the hard months following Appomattox. Although he proudly had worn Union blue during the war, Chance felt no pride in the government's policy of Reconstruction. Too often it was no more than thinly veiled theft and robbery—harsh punishment to break the backs of rebellious states. Already the refrain ''The South shall rise again'' was being voiced among the crushed Confederate States. To the gambler, the reaction was over-optimistic. Decades would pass before the South regained its former strength and beauty—if it ever did.

''We'll be journeying back downriver as soon as our riverboat arrives in Saint Louis,'' Anne continued.

Chance took another sip from the steaming cup. "New Orleans will be my own destination when my side-wheeler, the *Wild Card,* docks."

"The *Wild Card?*" Anne's gold-flecked eyes widened in surprise. "Why, we're booked aboard the *Wild Card.*"

The gambler smiled. Luck perched firmly on his shoulder. Just when he thought this comely angel of mercy was about to take wing before he had sufficient time to make her acquaintance, he discovered that he would be the man captaining her flight.

Well, almost, he mentally conceded. Bertram Rooker was the *real* captain aboard the paddlewheeler. However, he *was* the sole owner and proprietor of the *Wild Card;* and more important at the moment was the fact that he and Anne Walsh would have more than enough time to get to know each other on the long, leisurely journey down the Mississippi River.

"Riverboat owner? How does a man come to own a sternwheeler?" Anne asked while she refilled his cup from a small silver pot set to one side of the tray.

"Sidewheeler," the gambler corrected. "As for other men, I'm not certain how they came by their steamers, but in my case, I won the *Wild Card* in a poker game."

"Poker game?" Anne's eyes went wide again. "Then you have a bit of the wagering spirit in your blood, Mr. Shar— Chance?"

He chuckled. "I guess you could put it that way. By profession I'm a gambler, and I prefer to work the river. Although, if the stakes are interesting enough, I'm willing to let a game call me elsewhere."

"Not just the owner of a paddlewheeler, but a riverboat gambler—you're decidedly not an average, mundane businessman, Chance Sharpe." She settled back into the chair's cushions and stared at him.

Although he could not detect approval in her tone, he did notice indisputable interest in those alluring brown eyes and the hint of a smile that hung at the corners of her full-lipped mouth. *Yes,* he thanked his luck again, *Anne Walsh is definitely a young lady to get to know better.*

When he returned to the remainder of his meal, her questions led him through an abbreviated recounting of his life, beginning as a thirteen-year-old boy who ran away from his father's Kentucky farm to answer the call of the river. "By fifteen I discovered poker and have been playing ever since—on the Mississippi, in California—wherever men sit down, shuffle a deck, and place money on the table. Except for a brief try at college and an unexpected stint in the U.S. Army during the war, it's the only trade I've ever learned."

He capsulized his time in the army, concluding with the year he spent fighting Comanches and Kiowas in Kansas before the army gave him his walking papers. "A few days after I returned to civilian life, I won the *Wild Card* and have sailed aboard her ever since." He failed to mention that during the same time he had been accused of murder—twice—and robbery, and had almost been lynched by an overeager self-proclaimed posse in the Dakota Territory. Aside from keeping the *Wild Card* afloat, he had spent the majority of his time making certain he didn't end up dangling from a hangman's rope for crimes he didn't commit.

"Tell me about your ship, Chance," Anne asked.

The gambler started to correct her calling a riverboat a *ship* when a knock came from the room's door. Anne rose and answered it. A solidly built man, standing a full six feet tall, with graying temples and bushy black mustache entered when Anne stepped aside to admit him. The pants of his sharply creased gray suit hissed with each stride he took.

Behind the man came a woman in a satiny brown dress with white lace collar and cuffs. Except for the obvious years separating them, the woman with silver threads interwoven in her nut brown hair could have been Anne's sister. She wasn't, of course, Chance realized, but was Anne's mother. Which, in all probability, made the man Anne's father.

The last person to enter the hotel room was a young man no more than eighteen years old. *Warren,* the gambler recalled Anne's younger brother's name.

To confirm his suspicions, Anne held out an arm and introduced; "Chance, I would like you to meet my father, Graham Walsh, my mother, Rachael, and my brother Warren."

There was a round of the expected handshaking and an unexpected profusion of sincere gratitude from the husband and wife for the gambler's quick thinking and equally quick rescuing of their daughter from two cutthroats.

"I realize that you are still recovering from a foully inflicted wound and require your rest, which we will allow you to return to, if you'll bear with me for one minute longer," Graham Walsh eventually said. "Your physician, Dr. Craighead, has led me to believe that there is a possibility that you will be up and around this evening. If so, my family and I would be honored if you would allow us to entertain you at dinner tonight."

"It is I who would be honored," Chance accepted the invitation.

Before he or the others could say another thing, Anne spoke up. "The doctor *did* say that Chance was supposed to rest. It would be best if we let him do just that."

She lifted the tray from his lap and shooed her family from the room. When she reached the threshold, she glanced back at her patient. "I'll call on you later this afternoon to see if you've recovered enough for dinner."

Chance nodded, and watched her close the door. He smiled as he slid back down into the bed, pulled the covers snugly under his chin, and closed his eyes. He had let Anne get away without asking her what she knew about Chester Ludd and Morris Bigelow or why the two men had attempted to kill her in the alley.

It didn't matter, he realized as he sank into a peaceful sleep. There would be time enough later, when they were aboard the *Wild Card*.

FOUR

Chance's heart beat at triple time when he stepped from the taxi and handed the cabbie five crisp one-dollar bills. He turned from the hack and started down the long wharf. His temples resounded with the runaway pounding in his chest when his gaze homed to the end of the wooden pier.

The majestic lady of the river who awaited him was like no other among the mile of riverboats that lined St. Louis's docks. This one belonged to *him!*

And I almost missed the sailing of my own paddle-wheeler! the gambler mentally reprimanded himself. A friendly game of poker in the hotel's sitting room and a five-hundred-dollar pot had detained him. The outrageously exorbitant promise of five dollars to the cabbie had been the only incentive to insure a direct and speedy flight through the city's streets. Now the hack driver's petty theft didn't matter; he was reunited with the only true love in his life—the *Wild Card!*

Three hundred and fifty feet from her bow to her stern, the *Wild Card* was a luxury steamer that rivaled the legendary *Eclipse* that had churned the Mississippi's muddy waters with her massive paddlewheels before the Civil War. On the outside, Chance admitted to himself, the *Wild Card,* aside from being bigger, differed little from the other riverboats that she berthed beside. She was painted white, except for two black

25

smokestacks, and was decorated on every deck with elaborate jigsaw work, or *gingerbread,* as it was often called. However, inside—especially in the saloon or main cabin—the *Wild Card* was a floating palace of opulence complete with crystal chandeliers and stained-glass skylights.

Nor were the staterooms to be overlooked. Each was at least ten feet by ten feet, with many measuring a luxurious fifteen by fifteen. Those who had ever sailed aboard another steamer soon learned to appreciate the *Wild Card*'s grand design and the impressive fourteen miles an hour she averaged in open water.

Five long blasts from a steam whistle atop the side-wheeler hastened the gambler's steps. The steam's strident cry was the last warning for all passengers to come aboard. Chance crossed the forward gangplank in a full run as roustabouts swung the loading ramp away from the pier and onto the paddlewheeler, nearly costing him his balance and depositing him unceremoniously on his backside.

Laughter greeted the gambler when his boots touched the boards of the *Wild Card*'s main deck. His cool, steel blue eyes shot up, seeking the source of the loud guffaws. A young man dressed in the black cap, coat, and breeches of a riverboat pilot clutched his belly with his left hand as though afraid the force of his merriment would somehow displace his innards.

"It's always nice to hear the warm welcome of a friend, Henri." Chance made no attempt to hide the touch of disgust in his voice. "A man would think that he might be able to receive a bit more consideration on *his own* boat than being treated like a stowaway trying to leap aboard a steamer at the last moment."

For an instant Henri Tuojacque's face sobered to a mask of mock distress—only for a moment. The gleam in the young pilot's jet eyes could not be contained.

He burst into laughter once again as he strode beside the gambler and heartily slapped his friend on the back.

"I mean no disrespect to the proprietor of this magnificent vessel, nor would you have suffered such indignities had my gentle hands been at the wheel. But with Bert working the sticks, I was certain that he would find some means of reminding you that you were once more on the Mississippi and not still hunting the deer in the Dakota Territory." Henri's voice betrayed a slight hint of his French heritage.

Chance's gaze rolled upward to the pilothouse for a moment. "I'll discuss our Captain Rooker's manners in private with Bert later. Right now, I want to know how the *Wild Card* has fared these last months?"

In truth, he realized, there was nothing he could say to Bert about the way the captain handled the steamer. Once at the wheel, a pilot was the undisputed ruler of a paddlewheeler; no one, not even the owner, could question his actions. For the moment, Chance would simply have to endure the crusty old captain's small joke. Later, he would find a way to repay it.

"As you can see, the *Wild Card* is fine. There is nothing else to tell. Bert has run her as if she were his own." Henri swept his arm around the vessel as the two men climbed a stairway to the riverboat's second level, the boiler deck. "What I want to hear about is your deer hunt. I've never known a man to spend months tracking down a buck."

"Another time when I have a few days to tell all the details," Chance replied. "I really would like to take a long, hard look at the *Wild Card*."

The deer to which Henri referred was not one of the moments in the gambler's life that he wished to remember. He and a roustabout had left the riverboat to hunt fresh meat meant to restock the sidewheeler's pantry. A grizzly bear, searching for its own fresh meat, had killed the roustabout and left Chance wounded and lost in the Dakota wilds. To return to the river and the *Wild Card*, he had dodged a lynch party, cleared himself of murder and robbery charges for which he had been falsely accused, and fought his way across the Dakota Territory and half the Sioux nation.

"I understand." When Henri's expression grew somber this time, there was no doubt of the young pilot's sincerity. "Chance, it *is* good to have you back. When we found what was left of the roustabout who went with you into the woods, we thought that you had been killed, too."

"Believe me, Henri, it *is* good to be back."

"After you've had your look-see, meet me in the main cabin and I'll buy you a welcome-home drink." The six-foot pilot reached out and squeezed the gambler's shoulder.

Chance nodded and smiled. "I'll do that, Henri—especially since you're buying."

As the pilot moved forward along the boiler deck's railed guard walk, Chance pulled a saber cigar from inside his coat and lit it. His smile widened when he exhaled a thin, blue stream of smoke. The strength of the *Wild Card*'s massive engines vibrated through the deck's boards and tingled the soles of his feet. Henri was right; he *was* home again. And he intended to give himself the luxury of a casual stroll around his floating estate before he once again settled into the responsibilities of being a riverboat owner.

A dusky evening with the western sky aglow from the last fading reds and oranges of sunset hung over the river before Chance at last turned his gaze from the *Wild Card*'s magnificence. Soon it would be time for the pilot's shift to change. He had promised to raise a glass with Henri in the saloon. Little time remained to keep that promise before the Frenchman had to climb his way to the uppermost deck and relieve Captain Bert Rooker of the wheel.

After Bert came down from the pilothouse, the gambler was certain the captain would want to thoroughly discuss the business occurrences during Chance's long absence. Inwardly Chance groaned. Familiarizing himself with all that had happened while he was away was something that had to be done sooner or later. However, tonight he wished that it could be later. He was back on the river and wanted to savor it. The only work he felt willing to perform was to shuffle and deal cards—and maybe rake in a few pots.

Resigned to the fate that awaited him for the majority of the evening, Chance used thumb and forefinger to flip the still smouldering butt of a cigar outward over the steamer's rail. Like a meteor trailing a fiery red tail, it arced through the air to fizzle out when it struck the water's rippled surface. He had to make the best of what time remained to him. With luck, he could share one, maybe two, drinks before Bert's arrival.

The gambler turned and walked toward the forward portion of the boiler deck. There he found double doors that led to the paddlewheeler's main cabin. Using both arms to part the swinging doors, he entered.

A deafening cheer and thundering applause greeted him. Together, every man and woman inside the elegant saloon stood and began clapping. A white banner painted in big, black letters that proclaimed **Welcome Back Chance** unfurled from the spacious room's arched ceiling. Through the din of revelry he heard the distinct pop of champagne corks saluting his entrance.

From out of the standing crowd of passengers came a man who stood five feet eight. Thick tufts of salt-and-pepper pushed from beneath the captain's hat tugged firmly on his head. Bushy muttonchop sideburns of the same hue almost concealed the man's ears and half his square jaw.

"Bert, what's going on here?" the gambler greeted Captain Rooker. "What's this all about?"

"It's about getting your ornery backside back aboard the *Wild Card* where it belongs." Bert's gravelly voice made itself heard even over the cheering crowd. "Every passenger on this boat knows what you've been through these past months. Me and the crew asked them to join us in welcoming you back."

Before Chance could answer, Katie McArt, the *Wild Card*'s fiery-haired bartender, dressed in a satiny gown of forest green, wove through the crowd, carrying two glasses of champagne. After a quick kiss for the gambler's cheek, she handed him one of the glasses and raised her own. "Welcome back to where you belong, Chance."

Lifting the glass of bubbling wine, Chance held it toward Katie, then Bert, and finally toward the crowd within the main cabin. He then drank deeply. In response, the passengers cheered and applauded once more before draining their own glasses. As the clapping and shouts of well-wishing began to fade, the band struck up a gentle waltz. Katie's emerald eyes lifted to Chance.

"Would you be thinking it bold of me to be asking you for this first dance?" The Irish coursing through the beautiful redhead's veins was more than apparent in her accent.

"Katie darling, the honor will be mine," the gambler answered, tossing down the last of the champagne and handing the empty glass to Bert.

Slipping her arm through the hook in his, Katie walked with him to the dance floor. *It is good to be home*, he thought for the hundredth time since setting foot back aboard the *Wild Card*. Then as his arm went about Katie's slender waist, all his thoughts focused on his alluring companion.

FIVE

An hour into his homecoming celebration, Chance glimpsed Anne Walsh out of the corner of an eye. Turning, the gambler's gaze traveled across the long, narrow gallery of the paddlewheeler's main cabin. A smile touched his lips; in the excitement of the unexpected welcoming, he had forgotten that his attractive young nurse and her family were booked aboard the *Wild Card*.

With white gown flowing around her, Anne sat beside her mother, Rachael, on a richly brocaded divan in the ladies' section of the saloon. Demurely her gaze shifted from the other women at the rear of the main cabin to the revelers who boisterously occupied the two dining sections and the dance floor that separated them. A smile of anticipation uplifted the corners of her mouth when her eyes alighted on the gambler.

Chance's own smile widened. He had no intention of ignoring the quiet plea that he read in Anne's expression—to be rescued from the gossip of the middle-aged matrons who surrounded her.

"Chance."

Bert Rooker's gravelly voice intruded into the gambler's thoughts of leading Anne Walsh onto the dance floor. He glanced to his left to see the captain approach. A glass of bourbon replaced the champagne that Bert had last held in his hand.

"I hate to interrupt your festivities, but we need to talk business," Bert said as he reached his friend's side. "A lot of things have happened aboard the *Wild Card* since you went and got yourself lost in the Dakota Territory. If we can get away to my cabin, I think that I can cover most of them in a half hour . . . an hour, at most."

"Bert, I'll be right with you," Chance replied, holding up a hand to waylay the captain. "I just noticed a young lady who I promised a dance earlier."

Before Bert could protest, Chance pivoted and started toward the ladies' section. With only one long stride toward his destination, he halted. A bewildered expression clouded his face. Anne and her mother were gone! The sofa that had held them was now empty!

"Damn!" The frustrated curse slipped softly between his lips while his gaze scanned the crowd packed within the saloon. Neither of the Walsh women was in sight.

"Chance, we really need to talk." Bert moved to the gambler's side again. "I promise it won't take long. You'll be back to this shindig before anyone misses you."

Chance looked back at his friend and nodded in acceptance. Talking business with Bert came in a poor second to dancing with Anne Walsh.

"Probably the biggest change since you wandered off into that forest is a new pilot I hired in New Orleans just before we came upriver. Ted Stower is his name—been working the sticks since before the war," the captain began. "Then I picked me up a cub about a month back."

"Cub?" Chance asked, uncertain what his friend meant.

"A cub . . . an apprentice," Bert explained. "He goes by the name Gary Eakin."

Chance didn't question Bert's acceptance of an apprentice; it was one of the privileges of every pilot aboard every steamer in the country. As was collecting and keeping the exorbitant fees—usually amounting to thousands of dollars—a cub paid an experienced pilot for teaching him the ways of the river and the paddle-wheelers that sailed it. A riverboat owner had no say in the matter, nor did he receive a cut of the fees. However, he was expected to provide an apprentice with room and board.

"We've managed to pick up quite a few new shipping accounts in the past month," Bert continued as he walked toward the forward exit to the main cabin.

Chance half listened to his friend. His gaze still searched for Anne Walsh. The young woman was nowhere to be found.

Selecting two blue wooden chips and a single red, Chance tossed them into the pot at the center of the green felt–covered table. The twenty-five dollars paid for his last hole card in a hand of seven-card stud. The game was not to his liking, but as the evening stretched to the early hours of morning and the crowd of revelers dwindled, only one table of poker players remained in the saloon.

The dealer, a crystal merchant from New York, lifted the deck and passed a card each to the last three players remaining in the hand. Chance used a thumb to lift a corner of the card that landed before him—a knave of spades. Teamed with the two jacks lying faceup on the table, Chance's hand tallied to three jacks and trash.

His eyes lifted and briefly examined the two other hands challenging his. The crystal merchant had a pair of queens showing, and Bill Hicks, a St. Louis newspaperman, displayed two sevens.

The odds said that Chance should match and raise the five the dealer added to the pot. However, there was more to poker than the ability to read pieces of pasteboard and calculate odds. A successful gambler also read men. A hungry glint in Bill Hicks's gray eyes spoke louder than his pair of sevens. Chance folded.

Seconds later, Hicks called the bet and flipped over four deuces to beat the dealer's queens and fives. His hands shot out to eagerly scoop in the pot.

"I like this game." The reporter grinned as the cards were passed to him for the deal. "Let's give it another go."

While the six other players anted one-dollar white chips, Chance raked his remaining chips from the table and bade the others a good night. In a matter of two hours he had lost three hundred dollars—a far from auspicious return to the *Wild Card*'s gaming tables. Rather than throwing good money after bad, he accepted the fact that the cards weren't with him this night. Luck changed; tomorrow evening it might sit solidly on his shoulder.

Tugging the collar of his coat high, the gambler crossed the gaming section of the main cabin and walked through the forward doors. The January night felt crisp and cold. To the east, the constellation of Leo the Lion was rising to take its place among the diamond-bright stars of the heaven.

Chance extracted the last saber from his coat, struck a match, and sucked at the cigar until its end glowed cherry red. He flipped the match away and began to walk. The edge to the air felt crisp—alive. The brandy awaiting in his stateroom would taste twice as good after a quick stroll around the boiler deck. Then he could sink into the comfort of his own bed—a luxury long missed while in Dakota.

A thin stream of smoke trailing from the corners of his mouth, Chance turned to the right and began to walk toward the aft of the steamer's second deck. A row of white-painted doors formed a blur on his right. Unlike other riverboats on the Mississippi, the *Wild Card*'s staterooms had doors that opened onto the boiler deck's guard way as well as into the saloon.

The gambler glanced at the names of the states painted in black on each of the doors. Behind one of them slept Anne Walsh. Tomorrow he would have to check the passenger roster to find exactly which one.

At the rear portion of the deck, Chance paused by the railing and stared out at the inky water. Here and there he caught a hint of the boat's powerful side wheels' wake when the river's surface glinted with reflected stars.

He drew another puff from the cigar and let the smoke explode from his mouth in a minor cloud. Even with the relentless pounding of the *Wild Card*'s engines, there was a certain peace on the Mississippi that he had never been able to find elsewhere. Other men might deem a life spent in constant motion lunacy—a world in which a man's roots could never be sunk firmly into the soil. For the gambler, no other life was conceivable. This riverboat—*his* riverboat—was a palace adrift on the streams of adventure. To live out his years attached to a single parcel of land would have been akin to placing a revolver's muzzle to his temple, cocking the hammer, and pulling the trigger.

Chance didn't deny the monotony of river travel. More often than not, the majority of men and women who rode aboard a paddlewheeler simply found the journey boring. Chance escaped the tedium by retreating into his cabin and sampling the ever-increasing library of first editions that he collected to fill a floor-to-ceiling bookcase that covered one wall of his stateroom.

"Chance?" a feminine whisper called to him. "Is that you, Chance?"

The gambler turned to find Anne Walsh standing ten feet behind him. She hugged a dark wool coat close to her diminutive form.

"Anne?" Chance answered her. "I thought you had retired hours ago."

"I had, but I couldn't sleep. The hammering of the engines kept me awake." She stepped forward to lean against the rail beside him. "I heard footsteps pass my stateroom and glanced out. I thought it was you."

"I'm glad you peeked out. Company is always welcomed." Chance smiled at her.

"You seemed to have more than enough company tonight," she answered with an undercurrent of something in her voice that the gambler couldn't identify. "Your crew definitely seems to like you."

He chuckled. "Well, at least none of them have tried to kill me—lately."

Apparently she didn't see the humor in his comment. When she spoke, there was a somber tone to her voice that was incongruous with the question she asked. "Are you just out walking?"

Arching an eyebrow, the gambler tried to study her features in an attempt to discern what was bothering the young woman. The night was too dark to see more than her silhouette. "Actually, I was on my way to my cabin for brandy. Would you care to join me?"

"Chance, a woman of proper breeding is taught to believe a man has other matters on his mind than a glass of brandy when he invites a lady into his room."

Although the words were a definite rebuff, Chance detected no hint of reprimand in her tone. His puzzlement over her strange behavior grew. This was not the effervescent Anne Walsh who had nursed him back from the grave.

"To keep everything *proper,* we could leave the door to my room open," he suggested. "No one could question our intent then."

She didn't reply. Instead, she turned and stared out into the night.

"Or you might prefer a stroll around the *Wild Card?*" he tried again.

"No," she finally said. "The brandy sounds better."

Offering her his arm, he escorted her forward. When he opened the door to his cabin, he left it gaping and followed her inside. "Wait here, and I'll get a light."

Through the room's darkness he moved by memory to his desk and lit an oil lamp. "There, that's better." He glanced at Anne. Worry furrowed her forehead. "Anne, is there something you want to talk with me about?"

She shook her head. "No, but I would like the brandy."

Chance tilted his head and lifted his eyebrows as he turned to the desk. He uncorked a crystal decanter and poured brandy into two snifters. With one glass in each hand, he once more faced the young woman.

Just in time to see her close the stateroom door. Without her eyes lifting to him. She tugged off her coat and placed it over the back of a chair. Beneath, she wore the white gown he had glimpsed her in earlier.

"Beautiful," he said. "I was on my way to tell you that you looked beautiful this evening when I was detoured by the *Wild Card*'s captain." He held out a glass to her.

She accepted the brandy, started to take a sip, then laid the glass aside atop a small round table standing beside her. "Chance, I didn't come here for this brandy. To tell the truth, I don't care for anything stronger than sherry.''

The gambler frowned. "Then you *do* want to talk with me about something. Does it have to do with the attack in the alley?''

She shook her head again as she took his drink from his hand and placed it beside her own untouched brandy. For an instant, her eyes darted to the brass bed that filled a corner of the stateroom, then they returned to him. "I'm not sure how to say this without making myself appear to be some brazen woman of the world.''

Still uncertain what she was trying to get at, he interjected, "I would never think that of you.''

"I hope not.'' Doubt tinged her gold-flecked eyes. "Chance, I came here for one reason—to be with you.''

He needed no further explanation. Her hesitancy and uncertainty were simply shyness. The Civil War had wrought many changes in a young nation, but the behavior of a woman toward a man—especially a man she desired—remained unaltered. The woman must always retain her passive role, never allowing her passion and needs to be glimpsed except behind the closed doors of a darkened bedroom.

Anne had overstepped the bounds of propriety by voicing her desire—a position that left her feeling uncomfortable and out of place. After she had just paid him the highest of compliments, distress was the last thing he wanted her to feel. The gambler reached out, took her hand, and squeezed it. A gentle smile moved over his lips as he tucked a finger beneath her chin and lifted her face to his. Leaning forward, he lightly kissed her full red lips.

That was all there was. When they parted, he gazed into her eyes, giving her time to reconsider and withdraw with no more than a memory of a moment of indiscretion to remind her of this night.

She made no retreat. Instead, she rose on her tiptoes so that her lips pressed firmly to his, then her mouth opened to him as his arms slid around her waist.

Time was of no essence to either of them. Nor was there a demanding purpose to the stroking caresses of their exploring hands. When a hook eased from its eye or a button slipped from a hole, it seemed to be more happenstance than design.

Yet, the same end was reached. Anne's gown slid from her shoulders and drifted to the floor like a white cloud. Eventually the layers of her undergarments fell away to join the gown until he gathered the summery warmth of her nakedness in his arms, lifted her, and placed her atop his bed.

Chance's steel blue eyes drank in her sleek beauty as he stood and began to shed his own clothing with alacrity. *Delicate* was the way he already thought of Anne. The impression was enhanced now as his gaze traveled over the soft, milky whiteness of her waiting body. She was like some fragile porcelain doll that might shatter if held too tightly.

Her breasts, small uptilted balls of flesh like firm, ripened apples, heaved while his eyes traveled down her body. Dark nipples atop those two mounds stiffened and stabbed into the air. Her smooth, flat stomach fluttered slightly as his gaze probed even lower to the dark downy patch between her parted thighs.

Stepping free of his breeches, Chance came to her, his body pressing her small form into the bed. Neither his nor her hand guided him when he found the moist entrance to their mutual pleasure. His hips arched downward.

For an instant there was resistance. A whimper of both desire and pain quavered over her lips.

Shoving to his elbows, Chance stared down at the woman beneath him. For the first time he fully understood Anne's doubt and uncertainty. She was as virginal as the white gown she had worn. "I didn't know," he said, unable to disguise his surprise at what she had given him.

"It doesn't matter—not any longer." Her arms encircled his back to draw his weight fully atop her. "I want this, Chance. If I didn't, I wouldn't have come here."

Her mouth and probing tongue cut short any reply that might have been on his own tongue. Her heels locked themselves around his legs, and she moved. And winced as her body learned to accommodate a man.

Only when he was certain that the last memory of his entrance had faded did his hips gently rock to match the undulating rhythm of her pelvis. It was with that same tenderness that his fingers and palms helped a girl discover the wants of her newfound woman's body. Slowly, ever so slowly, together they unlocked desires she had only dreamed of. And only when she had climbed to the peak of carnal pleasure did he sate his own needs.

Afterwards, when their entangled bodies separated and they rolled from each other, he let her drift into a soft sleep while he stood above her, savoring a glass of the brandy that had first brought her to his stateroom. His short acquaintance with Anne Walsh had been filled with surprises. If everything continued on its present course, it was going to be a very interesting trip downriver.

SIX

The *Wild Card*'s orchestra concluded a waltz and announced a fifteen-minute intermission. Chance took Anne's arm and led her to the ladies' section of the main cabin. There Rachael Walsh patiently awaited her daughter. After bidding the mother and daughter a pleasant night, the gambler watched the two depart through double glass doors at the rear of the saloon.

Chance slipped a shiny new gold pocket watch that he had purchased in St. Louis from his coat pocket—his vest pocket being occupied by a watch-fobbed .22-caliber Wesson derringer—and thumbed it open. *Right on time*, he thought, pursing his lips and cocking his head. Each night Rachael and Anne Walsh retired from the riverboat's festivities at exactly nine-thirty. The difference between the two women was that the daughter's night was far from over. At two she would slip from her stateroom to join the gambler in his cabin, hastening back to her own bed just as the horizon glowed rose with the coming dawn.

Chance did not endorse their secret rendezvous, but he didn't condemn them, either. A woman in Anne's position—young and unmarried—had a reputation to protect.

Bowing to the other ladies seated in the divans and chairs, the gambler walked to the casino section of the main cabin—the foremost area of the saloon—and ordered a shot of bourbon. When Katie McArt brought the drink, he leaned back against the dark-stained walnut bar and surveyed the gaming tables. Blackjack, roulette, keno, and poker all drew eager crowds; the house's take would be handsome tonight.

Among the faces of the unknown players, Chance's gaze picked out the familiar visage of Graham Walsh. Anne's father sat at what had become his favorite poker table, pondering the five cards fanned in his hand. The gambler shook his head. Why the elder Walsh had selected that particular table as being lucky eluded him. Graham had held only a few winning hands since the trip downriver had begun. On the other side of the coin, the man never wagered heavily, and considered his losses a small enough price to pay for an evening's entertainment. Chance would never argue with that philosophy.

Letting his gaze play over the crowd, the gambler couldn't locate Anne's younger brother, Warren. However, he did see the *Wild Card*'s newest pilot, Ted Stower, and Bert Rooker's cub, Gary Eakin, walk into the saloon through the forward entrance. He signaled the two men to join him at the bar. Both nodded and wove their way through the crowd of gamblers.

"Beer," Ted ordered, and Gary nodded for the same. The older Stower then looked at Chance. "Henri's just taken the sticks from us. It's been a long shift and my throat's as dry as Texas."

"Us?" Chance eyed Stower, a rail-thin, sharp-featured man with hair the yellow of rice straw. At first glance, Ted lacked the dashing appearance one usually associated with a riverboat pilot, a *prima donna* of the Mississippi. Closer inspection revealed the man's huge hands and the tight bundles of muscle that were his arms; both were needed to handle a steamer's wheel for hours on end.

"Mr. Stower allowed me in the wheelhouse with him," Gary Eakin spoke up. "The way I figure, any extra experience learning the river will get me that much closer to my license."

Chance nodded. Gary stood about five foot ten and still had the look and manner of a St. Louis dry-goods store clerk. With a twenty-year-old's eager attitude, his bright brown eyes, and usually disarrayed mop of brown hair, Gary presented the image of a young puppy willing to please a newfound master. In the apprentice's case, that master was the Mississippi River.

"Have you seen Captain Rooker this evening?" Ted asked after downing half his beer in a single gulp. When the gambler shook his head, the pilot shrugged. "Need to talk with him. Gary and I sighted a new pair of nasty-looking sandbars about two miles south of—"

Ted never finished his sentence. A cry of distress rose above the passengers' din within the saloon. The pilot's head snapped toward the forward doors, then twisted back to Chance. "It came from outside. Sounded like a man—in trouble!"

The gambler didn't question Stower. Instead, he pushed from the bar and shoved his way through the players in the casino. Once outside, heavy grunts and the scuffling of feet drew him to the right.

There, halfway to the bow portion of the boiler deck, Warren Walsh dodged a slash by a knife-wielding attacker. The instant the man's blade hand missed its mark, Warren's own arms shot out. His hands grasped his opponent's wrist in an attempt to immobilize that deadly weapon.

Although it was a valiant effort, Warren's tactic was also a mistake. The assailant's left hand remained free. This he employed like a hammer of flesh to the right side of Warren's face. The youngest of the Walsh family went down, sprawling with arms and legs wide, groaning as he struck the boards of the walkway.

For an instant the night-veiled attacker hesitated before wrenching the curved blade he brandished high into the air for the kill.

That second's delay was all Chance needed to free a .44-caliber Colt belly-gun tucked beneath the waistband of his trousers. With one hand he jerked the revolver up and fired at the man hovering over Warren.

Only the most astounding display of marksmanship and an astronomical portion of luck would have driven the shot home. The Colt with its inch-long sawed-off barrel was meant to be effective at a distance no greater than the width of a poker table. Beyond six feet, the weapon had no semblance of accuracy whatsoever.

However, the spent cartridge was far from wasted. The explosive thunder of black powder produced the effects Chance desired. The would-be killer glanced over a shoulder, saw the gambler and the crowd of shouting men who now followed him from the main cabin, realized the impossible odds, and ran.

Cocking the Colt with a thumb, Chance darted after the escaping man. Even by leaping over Warren's crumpled body, he was too late. As he reached the end of the boiler deck, the attacker tossed aside his blade and vaulted over the railing. The gambler could but stare below as the man hit the main deck on his feet, then ran and dived over the side of the riverboat. In the blinking of an eye, the man was lost in the inky water.

"Ted." Chance shouted back to the pilot following him. "Get topside and have Henri reverse course. I want to find that man. Gary, have the crew below light our running lights. If needed, see that every roustabout is carrying a torch. The brighter it is, the easier it will be to find him."

As the two men carried out his commands, Chance glanced back to the river. The night's blackness hid the assailant in his desperate swim for shore. *If the paddlewheels' backwash didn't suck him under,* the gambler thought as he eased the Colt's hammer down and tucked the gun back beneath his vest.

"Here's the blackheart's knife!"

A man's voice drew Chance's attention to the left. A cold spike drove up his spine when he saw the voice's owner stoop to pick up the blade.

"Don't touch that!" Leaning down, the gambler thrust out an arm and roughly shoved the man away from the knife. Balance lost, the knife's discoverer spilled onto the deck.

"What in hell is going on here?" The man stared up, blinking at the gambler in confusion. "I was only trying to help."

"Sorry, friend, but a neighborly act right now might have cost you more than you were willing to pay."

Waving the other onlookers back, Chance carefully lifted a wickedly curved wooden knife—a twin to the one that had nearly cost him his life in a St. Louis alley. Light from an open window of a stateroom ran along the razor-honed edge to reveal an uneven coating of a sticky, translucent amber substance. The gambler shivered in spite of himself. From its appearance, honey might have coated the blade, but he had no doubt that this was the same poison that had almost sent him to the grave. This time it had been intended for Warren Walsh rather than Anne.

"Chance, are you all right, man?" Graham Walsh called as he elbowed his way through the crowd gathered around the gambler. He supported a still dazed son with his left arm.

Chance glanced up and nodded.

"I saw what you did, and wanted to thank you for coming to Warren's aid," the elder Walsh continued. "I don't—"

The gambler held up a hand to silence the man. He then looked at Warren. "Tell me what happened."

Warren gingerly massaged the side of his face and shook his head. "I'm not certain. I had decided to try my hand at the roulette table when I discovered that I had left my wallet in my stateroom. I was on my way to retrieve it when that ruffian jumped me from the shadows. I'm certain he would have killed me had you not made such a timely appearance."

The gambler glanced around him. He couldn't even accurately judge the number of bystanders because of the darkness. It would have been easy for a man to go unnoticed, if he stood pressed flat against one of the stateroom doors. "Did you get a look at him?"

Warren nodded. "An ugly brute with a scar running from the left side of his forehead, downward across his left eye and ending at his upper lip. I'd never seen him before."

"Have any idea why he wanted to kill you?" Chance pressed.

Again the young man shook his head. "As I said, I'd never seen him until he attacked me."

"I was afraid of that." Chance released a long sigh and shook his head. "We've got Saint Louis all over again."

"What?" This from Graham Walsh.

Holding up the wooden blade, the gambler passed it to the older man. "Does this look familiar?"

"Damned filthy thing!" Even in the light filtering from the stateroom's open window, Chance could see Graham visibly pale as he held the knife in a shaking hand. Abruptly without warning, Graham pivoted and with a violent jerk of his arm angrily sent the wooden weapon sailing into the night. "What vile creature is doing this to my children?"

Chance stared at the water below, trying to locate the blade. Only the inky face of the Mississippi stared back at him. "I wish you hadn't done that. I would have liked the authorities to examine it."

"What good would it have done?" The elder Walsh's voice trembled as he spoke. Whether with indignity or fear, Chance couldn't determine. "The police in Saint Louis had the knife that almost killed you, but it didn't provide any answers. Why would anyone want to kill my son and daughter?"

"I was hoping that you might be able to shed some light on that," Chance replied.

"Me?" Outrage was now quite distinctive in Graham's expression. "Chance, I don't know what you're implying, but I assure you I know no more about these murderous attacks on my family than do Warren or Anne."

"I wasn't implying anything," Chance answered. "I was hoping for answers—"

Graham cut him off. "Then you're asking the wrong man. Try talking with the whoreson you let get away. He's the one who has the answers."

Chance let the man's remarks slip by. Graham was a father who had almost lost a son; he wasn't thinking clearly. "Why don't you take Warren to his room and tend that eye? It looks like it's beginning to swell."

Graham's gaze shifted to his son for a moment, then he looked back at the gambler. With a nod, he turned and helped Warren back along the guard way.

Chance watched the two depart, unable to shake the feeling that Graham Walsh knew more than he was saying.

* * *

"It's time to give it up, Chance," Bert Rooker said at the gambler's side while the two stood in the pilot-house staring at the river below.

"Bert's right," Henri Tuojacque added from behind the wheel. "We've been up and down these three miles of river at least ten times during the last two hours. We haven't seen any sign of the mysterious Mr. Treacher."

"If Treacher is his name," Chance answered while he continued to scan the Mississippi.

A comparison of the passenger list with those men still aboard the *Wild Card* had revealed a Billy Treacher to be missing. Treacher had taken passage as a "standee" in steerage on the main deck at the riverboat's last stop that afternoon. Bert recalled his boarding because of the scar on the left side of his face.

"Odds are he made it to the bank before we began our search," Bert said. "Or drowned."

Chance nodded with resignation. "You're both probably right. Henri, let's head toward New Orleans again."

As the pilot pulled a series of bells to inform the engineer below of a change in course, the gambler once more stared into the night, hoping for a glimpse of the would-be killer. He saw nothing but the shadowy distant banks. Like it or not, Billy Treacher would have provided no more answers than had Chester Ludd and Morris Bigelow.

SEVEN

With Bert Rooker working the sticks, the *Wild Card* swung to the middle of the Mississippi, did a one-hundred-eighty-degree turn, then gently edged port side to the end of a long, wooden wharf that jutted out into the water's current. Workers on the pier threw heavy mooring lines to roustabouts waiting on the sidewheel-er's main deck. They, in turn, secured the riverboat in her New Orleans berth.

Chance watched the docking activity from the bow of the boiler deck. The instant the *Wild Card*'s fore and aft gangplanks swung to the wharf, Bert let loose with five bellowing blasts from the steam whistle to signal the riverboat's arrival in the Crescent City.

The whistle was all that was needed to bring every deck of the paddlewheeler alive. Below in steerage, standees lifted carpetbags carrying their possessions or tossed burlap bags, holding similar treasures, over a shoulder and shoved toward the gangplanks like a herd of penned cattle escaping their confinement through a break in the fence. The chaotic scene only grew more confusing as roustabouts, ready to begin leave, attempted to clear the main deck and hold of their cargoes.

Nor was there much improvement on the boiler deck. The outer doors of staterooms flew open, and

passengers—loaded down with armfuls of baggage—
hastened to the stairways that led down to the main
deck.

The gambler smiled as he lit a saber and inhaled
deeply. In spite of America's romance with riverboats,
the truth remained that travel aboard a steamer, even
one as luxurious as the *Wild Card*, provided little more
than day upon day of monotony for most wayfarers.
Given an equal choice, most travelers would prefer the
speed of locomotives. However, the choice wasn't
equal: riverboat travel remained the cheapest mode of
transportation in the United States.

It won't always be that way, Chance realized. Rapidly, railroads were spreading their network of rails
from one coast to the other. The gambler could read
the writing plainly scrawled on the wall of the future.
Within his lifetime, passengers aboard steamers would
become a thing relegated to history books just as sure
as the keelboats that once dominated the Mississippi
were becoming a historical footnote.

If paddlewheelers were to survive—and that was a
big question in the gambler's mind—it would be by
hauling cargo alone. *That will be the end to this life
I've known for so long,* Chance thought with more than
a little self-pity.

He caught himself with a shake of his head. He was
beginning to sound like an old man. Decades remained
to this life. He'd be a silver-haired grandfather with
grandchildren on his knee before steamers became a
thing of the past.

"Chance," Anne called softly behind him. When he
turned to smile at her, she said, "I slipped away from
the others to speak with you alone."

The gambler stared at the young woman, uncertain
what was on her mind or what to say.

"I just wanted you to know that even if we never see each other again, I will always remember this trip. I know that there are no strings—"

"Anne!" Graham Walsh's voice boomed out. Halfway down the walkway the man hastened toward his daughter and the gambler with his wife and son following at his heels. "And Chance! I was hoping for the opportunity to see you before we left the ship. I wanted to express my gratitude once again for what you did for Warren that evening. I also wanted to make certain that you understood that anything I might have said that night stemmed from the tension of the moment."

Chance nodded. "It's understood. It's not an easy thing for a man to see another try to kill a member of his family."

It was Graham's turn to tilt his head in agreement. "But to make certain that there is no misunderstanding, my family and I would like to invite you to be a guest in our home next weekend."

"Graham, . . . Mrs. Walsh, . . ." the gambler began.

"Before you make up your mind," Graham interjected, "I must admit that my motive is more than a neighborly gesture. We are holding what is becoming one of New Orleans's major social events of the year. There'll be hunting, racing, balls—and, of course, poker. I'm hoping that you'll agree to attend and provide me with the opportunity of winning back a portion of the money that I've lost aboard your ship."

Chance didn't attempt to correct the man's calling the *Wild Card* a *ship*. Instead, he said, "I'm honored by the invitation, and I accept."

"Good, good, good," Graham said with a pleased grin. "We'll expect you there Friday afternoon. That will give me a chance to show you around before the other guests begin arriving.''

"Friday afternoon," Chance repeated.

Each member of the Walsh family then said their good-byes and shook the gambler's hand as they proceeded down the stairs to the main deck. All except Anne, who placed a hasty kiss on Chance's cheek and whispered, "Come even earlier, and I'll show you around our plantation." The impish gleam in her gold-flecked eyes left no doubt that she had more than sightseeing in mind during the gambler's stay.

Chance watched the family work its way to the lower deck; then a black man wearing a wide-brimmed straw hat adorned with a large blue flower caught his eye. The man sat in the driver's seat of a fringed taxi, waving at the gambler.

Homer? Chance wasn't certain whether to believe his eyes as he managed to move down the stairs, to the main deck, then across the gangplank. Before his series of misadventures in the Dakota Territory, he had kept the former slave and his hack on retainer. It was simpler to have the exclusive use of a taxi while in New Orleans than to try to maintain a horse and rig, especially since he was often absent from the city for long periods.

"Mr. Chance, you sure is a sight for these eyes!" The cabbie dipped his hat as the gambler approached. "Didn't think either me or Bad Bad here would ever see you again after Mr. Duwayne said you was et up by a bear."

"The bear thought I was too tough for dinner," Chance answered with a grin and a shake of his head, then asked, "Homer, what are you doing here, anyway? I haven't paid you in months."

"Makes me no never mind. When Mr. Duwayne's housekeeper Clarice says you was coming in on the

Wild Card, I had to come down here and make certain she wasn't lyin' through her teeth,'' Homer said, his grin flashing ivory against his ebony face. " 'Sides, I told myself, if'n you was alive, you might need fetchin' somewheres.''

"You told yourself right.'' Chance withdrew fifty dollars from his billfold and passed it up to the cabbie. "That puts you back on the payroll. Now, if you'll wait a few minutes I'll gather my things and be right back.''

"Homer A. Lincoln and Bad Bad ain't goin' nowheres except where you tell us,'' he assured the gambler as he stuffed the crisp green bills into his pants pocket. "We'll be waitin' right here for you.''

With a nod for the former slave and a pat on the rump for the dappled gray mare that Homer called Bad Bad, Chance hastened back aboard the *Wild Card.* Now that he had transportation, he had one call to make before New Orleans and he began to get reacquainted.

Clarice's eyes went saucer-round when she answered the door to the Duwayne home. An instant later, an ear-to-ear grin split her dark face. "If you wasn't so big, Mr. Chance, I reach up and give you a hug. Lordy, but it's good to see you looking as fit as a fiddle.''

"And very much alive,'' the gambler added as the maid admitted him to the home.

"Ain't no need me having you wait here while I announce to Mr. Philip that you done come,'' Clarice said as she snagged his arm and ushered him inside. "Mr. Philip's eatin' his dinner, and there's more than enough for a welcomed guest in this house.''

The housekeeper didn't release her hold on the gambler until she had pulled him into the dining room.

While Philip—the gambler's attorney and friend—and Chance said their greetings, shook each other's hands, and slapped each other's backs, Clarice set a place for the unexpected visitor. Chance didn't protest; he had tasted the black woman's cooking on more than one occasion.

"It ain't much, but there's plenty of it," she said as the gambler took his place at the table. "Eat all you want, and if there ain't enough, I'll cook up another mess of fish 'specially for you. You look like you done lost a pound or two, Mr. Chance."

The brown-haired attorney chuckled at the fuss his housekeeper made, but Chance merely followed the woman's advice and dug in to a meal of fried catfish that had been dipped in cornmeal batter, spicy tomato relish, sliced onions, hush puppies, and fried potatoes. Neither he nor Philip mentioned business until they retired with their overstuffed stomachs to the lawyer's den for coffee and cigars.

"You should go off and let everyone believe you were killed by a grizzly more often," Philip said as he took a file from his desk and handed it to his friend. "That's the profit the *Wild Card* made during your absence."

A low whistle came from Chance's lips when he opened the folder and read the tally of figures within. He arched an eyebrow and glanced up at the attorney. "Twenty-five thousand?"

"Twenty-five plus, actually," Philip replied. "If you'll remember, I wired you money while you were in Beltin, Dakota."

"Maybe I *should* lose myself more often." Chance passed the file back to Philip.

The attorney chuckled. "And if you want to get out of the riverboat business, I can get one hundred and seventy-five thousand for the *Wild Card*."

"I think I'll pass, but who would pay that much for my side-wheeler?"

"Several interested parties," Philip replied. "When word got out that you were dead, I received ten offers to buy the *Wild Card*. The highest was one hundred and seventy-five thousand dollars."

"Sounds like I've become more of a man of property than I realized," Chance said with an amazed shake of his head.

"Enough that I've drawn up a proposal on several propositions that I think you should consider investing in." Philip handed him another folder.

Which Chance handed right back. "Philip, I'm a gambler, have been all my grown life. I've no interest in investments. Money is a nice thing to have, but you have to remember that it's only a way of keeping score."

"Read my report. You pay me quite handsomely for things like this." Philip shoved the folder into the gambler's hand and refused to take it back. "By the way, before I forget, I've had your old suite reserved at the Hotel Burgundy. However, if you wish, you're welcome to stay here."

"Thank you, but my comings and goings don't correspond to those of a lawyer." Chance stood and offered his friend his hand. "Unless I can interest you in a night on the town, I'm going to say good-bye. I just wanted you to know I was alive and well."

For a moment Philip's expression lengthened, then he grinned widely. "A night on the town—why not. I've no cases in court tomorrow. Give me time to get a dress coat, and we'll see if we can find anything or any*one* to help warm this winter's night."

Chance nodded and watched his friend leave the room to retrieve a coat. Philip's comment about finding someone to warm the night brought an image of

Anne Walsh to the gambler's mind. He smiled; he already looked forward to seeing the young woman again, and he had left her less than three hours ago.

The Friday would come soon enough, he realized. At the moment, another delta lady awaited him—one called New Orleans.

EIGHT

"Quarters have been provided for your servant behind the main house," a butler announced as he opened the cab's door for Chance and motioned for two young boys dressed in green and white livery to gather the gambler's luggage.

"I ain't no servant." Homer grinned down at the somber-faced butler and tilted a frayed and weathered captain's cap decorated with a red rose in the man's direction. "However, if'n you requires it of me, I'd be more than happy to stay wherever they want to put me, Mr. Chance."

The gambler looked up at the cabbie and shook his head. "That won't be necessary, Homer. I'll be ready to leave Sunday afternoon, say at four o'clock."

"Sunday it is, then." Homer glanced down to make certain the luggage was free of the cab; then called out, "Gitup, Bad Bad."

While the hack rolled back toward the city, Chance followed the still unsmiling butler into a two-story antebellum mansion complete with whitewashed pillars lining its front. Anne stood grinning at the foot of a sweeping staircase that curved down from the second floor. She ran forward, stood on her tiptoes, and loudly kissed the gambler's lips.

"I thought you might have forgotten about coming early today," Anne said, her voice brimming with unrestrained delight. "I'm so glad you didn't. Father and Mother are still in New Orleans and won't be home for at least another two hours. I'll be the one who shows you around Ravenhill. When will you be ready? I have two horses saddled and waiting for us at the stable."

"I'm ready right now," Chance answered, slipping his arms around Anne's slender waist.

"Don't you think that you should introduce our guest before you drag him out horseback riding?"

Anne spun around and stared up the stairway. A woman, perhaps five years older than her, strode down the stairs. She tossed aside her coal black hair and eyed Chance. Her gaze then shot to Anne, and an amused smile uplifted the corners of her mouth.

"Aren't you going to introduce me, little sister?" she asked as she stopped in front of the couple.

"Elouise, I'd like you to meet Chance Sharpe. Mr. Sharpe owned the riverboat on which we returned from Saint Louis." The eagerness faded from Anne's tone. "Mr. Sharpe, this is my sister, Elouise."

"Miss Walsh." Chance bowed slightly.

"Owner of the riverboat and a gambler, if I remember correctly." Again Elouise's eyes shifted between the gambler and her sister. The amused smile seemed to twist into a smirk that said she knew exactly what had happened between the two aboard the *Wild Card*. "A romantic combination, Mr. Sharpe. I'm certain that it's turned more than one or two heads."

Before Chance could offer a reply, Anne said, "I was about to show Mr. Sharpe Ravenhill. Would you care to join us, Elouise?" The chill in her voice would have frozen a man dead in his tracks, had she used it on a male.

Elouise merely laughed. "I believe that I would be an unwanted cog in the wheel, sister dear. I think I overheard you mention to Mr. Sharpe that two horses were waiting in the stable. I wouldn't want to ruin your plans." She then turned to Chance. "I look forward to discussing your professions at dinner this evening."

Without another glance at either of them, she turned and disappeared into the immense mansion.

Anne took Chance's arm and tugged him toward the door. "Come on before she changes her mind. There is nothing more Elouise would like to do than ruin my plans for this afternoon."

That the gambler detected an undercurrent of sibling rivalry between the two sisters was understating the obvious. However, the reason for Elouise's cold shoulder was left unspoken as Anne hurried him to a long, low-slung rock building a quarter of a mile behind the main house. There, two grooms led saddled mounts from stalls and helped man and woman into their respective saddles.

"It's beautiful, don't you think?" Anne waved an arm before her, indicating the land on which they rode.

Except for the unmistakable boundaries of a bayou that pushed towering cypress trees toward the sky just beyond the mansion, Chance agreed with his young hostess. Even in the middle of winter, the gambler could well imagine the full beauty of the plantation when summer turned it brilliant green. He could almost catch the scent of magnolias in the air and see the delicate crepelike flowers of massive bougainvillea vines. That Graham Walsh had managed to hang onto this prized parcel of land after the end of the war seemed more miraculous with each stride of their mounts. Land-hungry and profit-greedy scalawags and carpetbaggers certainly had attempted to legally steal Ravenhill away from Walsh.

"What I want you to see is just beyond that stand of pines." Anne pointed to a dense line of long-needled evergreens on the other side of the field they crossed. She used a quirt she held in her right hand to sharply pop the rump of the chestnut filly she rode. The horse lunged forward in an easy gallop.

Chance's heels tapped the flanks of his own gray mount, urging the gelding after the young woman. He stared in puzzlement when Anne finally drew to a halt before a weather-beaten old barn that was strangely incongruous with the rest of the well-kept structures he had seen on Ravenhill.

Anne laughed when she noticed his bewilderment. Without explanation, she slid from her sidesaddle, walked to the barn's double doors, and threw them open. "It's wonderful, isn't it?"

"This barn?" Chance asked, uncertain what he was supposed to answer.

"You don't strike me as a man who would judge a book by its cover, Chance Sharpe." Anne led her chestnut inside and tied its reins to one of the barn's support columns. "It isn't the exterior that's important, but what's inside." She waved an arm to mound upon mound of silky, golden rice straw piled within. "Can you think of a more exciting bed for a man and a woman to spend a nippy January afternoon in?"

She turned to the gambler, her gold-flecked eyes glinting in the sunlight. With his cool blue eyes on her, she began to unfasten the buttons and hooks of her bodice.

Chance needed no formal invitation to outline the plans Anne had in mind for the afternoon. Throwing his right leg over the gray's neck, he dropped to the ground and joined the alluring young woman inside the hay-filled barn.

"Mr. Sharpe, I've heard a lot about you, especially from my father. He's determined to win back some of the money he lost aboard the *Wild Card* this weekend." James Walsh, Anne's older brother, held out his left hand to the gambler.

"I'll do my best to make certain that doesn't happen." Chance shook the extended hand, ignoring the right arm that hung limply at the man's side. He remembered Anne's mentioning that James had lost use of an arm during the war. Like the gambler, James had donned Union blue during the bloody struggle.

"Later tonight when the men retire for cigars, billiards, and cards, I hope we'll have the opportunity to talk," James continued. "At the moment, I must help my parents greet our late-arriving guests. Will you excuse me?"

Chance nodded as the man exited the immensely oversized parlor. He then glanced around the room, surveying the groups of men and women who clustered here and there. "I'm beginning to understand what your father meant when he said this weekend was shaping into the social event of the year. That's General Taylor Waldrop by the fireplace."

"He's talking with Mason Treavor and Cal Rugg, who are both said to be prime candidates for high political office," Anne said. "And there's Samuel Cade. He's constructing a railroad line that extends all the way through Texas to the Mexican border."

Fifty couples in all, Chance remembered Anne's saying earlier, the cream of New Orleans's financial and political elite. He glanced away when a pair of narrowing eyes met his—the eyes of Judge Harlan Turner. It was apparent from the snow-haired jurist's expression that he recognized the gambler but could not place him. It was just as well: Turner had presided over the hearing that had cleared Chance of murder charges last summer.

"Anne, you look lovely tonight."

Chance glanced around to see Anne greeting a tall, dark-haired man, whom she introduced as Captain Michael Balinger. "Michael is our closest neighbor. His plantation is two miles away through the bayou."

"One can hardly call it a plantation," Balinger said. "I have a hundred acres on which I'm trying to cultivate a new strain of rice."

"Anne called you 'Captain.' Is it from the war?" Chance asked, estimating the man's age in the mid-thirties.

"The same period. I didn't serve on either side during the war," Balinger answered. "I was captain of a schooner at that time."

Someone across the room waved and caught Balinger's eye. Excusing himself, he joined an elderly couple. Anne's gaze followed him, then she looked back at Chance. "He's quite handsome, don't you think?"

"I don't notice that sort of thing—in men," he replied, winking at her.

She grinned and began escorting him around the room to make the necessary introductions. Bankers, shipping magnates, senators, and investors—he had heard of each hand he shook. And with each greeting face that smiled back at him, his doubts as to why Graham Walsh had invited him to this impressive gathering grew. Was it because the elder Walsh detected his younger daughter's interest in him? Or did the man hope to spice up his festivities with a professional gambler? Either way, Chance didn't care: it was going to be an interesting weekend. And a profitable one if the cards were with him.

Anne was in the process of introducing him to Seymour Jackson, a New Orleans mayoral hopeful, when the butler stepped into the room and announced that dinner was served. Anne slipped an arm through his, and they took their places in an opulent dining room

that had three candle-lit crystal chandeliers and a floor
of mirror-polished pink marble.

Fresh oysters from the Gulf began a fare that in-
cluded pheasant, shrimp, roasted pork, lobster, and a
variety of spicy Cajun dishes. A roll of thunder from
outside seemed perfectly timed to announce the flam-
ing dishes of bananas Foster the five servants brought
in atop silver trays.

Graham Walsh glanced over a shoulder to a line of
three French doors at one end of the dining room.
Lightning flashed in the distance, silhouetting the tops
of wind-stirred bald cypress trees. "It appears that
we're in for a bit of a blow tonight. I hope it passes
before the morning. I'd hate for rain to ruin our sched-
uled hunt."

"What will we be going after tomorrow, Graham?"
This from a man Anne identified as Charles Kinsing-
ton, an influential merchant.

"Boar." Graham turned back to his guests. "My
boys sighted a big one a few weeks back—a real tusker
that will make a grand trophy for the man who brings
the brute down. Of course, other game abounds for
those seeking tamer sport."

The elder Walsh chuckled—a sound that was echoed
by the majority of the men seated around the table.
Chance merely smiled. Hunting for sport did not ap-
peal to him. The countless times he had hunted in his
life had been for one purpose—food.

"It's the boar for me," Michael Balinger said. "A
big tusker's broken into my feed shed two—"

Lightning flashed and a peal of deafening thunder
crashed, drowning the man's words. All three pairs of
the French doors flew inward, driven by a howling
wind. Heavy drops of rain sparkled in the candlelight
an instant before the whipping wind extinguished the
chandeliers, leaving the dining room in darkness.

"Carlton," Graham Walsh called to his butler above the nervous tittering of the women within the room. "Carlton, get those doors and bring fresh candles."

"Yes . . ."

Startled gasps—from the men as well as the women—filled the dining room.

Chance's head jerked around to find the source of the guests' distress. Like a ghostly apparition, a small, half-naked figure, backlit by the jagged bolts of lightning that streaked through the storm boiling in the night sky, stood in a wide-legged, defiant stance at the threshold of the middle pair of doors. The wind tore at its shoulder-length hair, sending the black strands writhing like living serpents.

Although clothed only in a long breechclout that flapped just above the figure's knees, the gambler was unable to discern whether it was male or female. The silhouetting flashes of lightning, darkness of its skin, and the inky night combined to camouflage the mysterious intruder's sex.

As Chance and the rest of those gathered around the richly laden dining table stared on, the figure's right arm raised and pointed directly at the gathering's host, who sat at the head of the table.

"Graham Walsh, your eyes meet the ghost of the past."

The voice that came from the apparition's lips was dry and broken. Each word was deliberately pronounced as though formed by a tongue unfamiliar with the language it was forced to use.

"Hear the tortured cries of the souls I embody. They scream their agony in the wind." Another sudden gust of wind blasted into the room as though in sympathy with the figure. "Hear the curse placed upon your head by those souls, Graham Walsh. Know that the time approaches to pay for your transgressions against the tormented dead.''

Indian? Negro? Without light, Chance couldn't be certain.

"A week remains to you, Graham Walsh. But before the curse is complete and your debt fully extracted, you will taste the suffering of the souls who writhe in this breast. Before you suck your last breath, you shall see every member of your family precede you to the grave!''

A whimpering gasp shuddered from Walsh's solid body. "No, no! It can't be!''

"A week, Graham Walsh, and then your cries will join the howling of the damned!''

An actinic, blue-white sheet of lightning devoured the sky, its harsh glare flooding the room. Thunder boomed like an exploding howitzer. Then there was the driven pounding of falling rain.

"He's gone!'' a woman shouted in terror.

Chance blinked and stared at the French doors; they were empty. Pushing from his chair, he darted across the room to stand in the pelting rain and stare across the well-manicured lawn. Nothing! He saw no sign of the man—or woman—who had been here but an instant ago. Only the storm-bent cypresses of the bayou met his eyes. No living thing could disappear that quickly.

No living thing! The phrase echoed in his mind.

"The doors, sir,'' Carlton the butler called to him. "Would you assist me?''

Chance did, securely locking the glass doors against the storm's raging fury. Seconds later, a line of servants entered with fresh candles; and within another few minutes they had once more lit the chandeliers overhead.

The gambler's gaze moved over the faces of the guests. Shock, bewilderment, fear, terror—he saw it all in their expressions. Worse was the sickly pale visage of Graham Walsh. The man's gaze lay locked to the center pair of doors as though he still stared upon the uninvited visitor.

NINE

"My father has asked that I take his place during the hunt today," James Walsh announced to the crowd of fifty men who sat astride mounts outside the plantation's stable.

Although none of the guests commented, Chance read the doubt written on their faces as Graham's elder son stepped into a stirrup and swung to the back of a thick-chested black gelding. Shortly after last night's unsettling visitation, a visibly shaken Graham had announced that he suddenly felt ill. The man had retired to his room and hadn't been seen since.

Not that the gambler could fault him for his reaction. Any man, including Chance Sharpe—who placed no faith in supernatural "haints" and apparitions from beyond the grave—would have been taken with an abrupt case of the jitters had that grotesque figure stood, pointed a finger at him, and declared that he and all the members of his family would die within a week. Curses were usually born of human mouths with human mind and hands ready to see that the prophecies of doom are fulfilled.

And someone definitely wants to harm the Walsh family, Chance thought. There was no way that Graham, locked away in his room, could deny that. Not after the attempts on Anne's and Warren's lives. And now the mysterious promise of death thrown in the man's face before a dining room packed with guests . . .

"Bring out the hounds!" James called to the kennel keepers.

As two men opened a gate to a large wooden pen, releasing thirty barking and yapping spotted dogs, another man walked to James's side and handed him a double-barreled shotgun. James wedged the weapon beneath his lifeless right arm, then took a handful of shells from the man and stuffed them into the pocket of his coat. To Chance's amazement, the eldest of the Walsh offspring never touched the reins that lay across his mount's neck as he led the hunting party toward the dense forest skirting the bayou.

"He trains his horses to respond to voice commands and the pressure of his knees," a rider said beside the gambler. "It appears quite miraculous, but in actuality the feat differs little from the process Texas cowboys use to train their cutting horses."

Chance barely contained a grimace when he glanced at the voice's owner—Judge Harlan Turner!

"It's a fine morning for a hunt, don't you agree, Mr. Sharpe?" The jurist looked up at the clear blue sky and smiled. "After last night's frog-strangler, I'd've thought that we'd have rain this morning. I guess there's no predicting delta weather."

"Good morning, Judge." Chance could think of nothing else to say to the man he had hoped to avoid.

Judge Turner's eyes rolled to the gambler, and he smiled. "Then you do remember me?"

"It's hard to forget a man who held one's life in his hands," Chance conceded, "even if only for a few minutes."

"I suppose what you say is true." The judge glanced at the other riders as they urged their horses into an easy lope, following James Walsh into the woods.

Turner kept his mount at a walk. "However, if you're sitting on the opposite side of the bench, you sometimes forget. Faces begin to blur into one another. That's the way it was last night when I first saw you, Mr. Sharpe. I was certain I had seen you before, but I couldn't place where. This morning I remembered. You were the riverboat gambler who was charged with Wilson Morehead's murder. Some ragtag sheriff from Texas testified that his own brother had shot down the stockbroker, if I recall the case."

"Your memory's correct," the gambler answered, not mentioning that although Turner had dropped the murder charges, the judge had levied heavy fines for several trumped-up minor charges surrounding Chance's escape from a New Orleans jail—an escape required to track down the real killer.

"You've moved up in the world since last we met, haven't you, Mr. Sharpe?" The judge arched a white eyebrow and stared at the gambler.

Chance clenched his teeth to contain the curses that stood poised to leap from his tongue tip. Were Turner not so influential, he would have told the man exactly what he thought of that last comment. However, the New Orleans police and Chance Sharpe had never been accused of being friends. The gambler might one day stand before Turner again. There was no need to predispose the man's attitude to him.

"I just wanted you to know that at least one of Graham's guests was aware of your background, Mr. Sharpe," the judge continued. "And that man is keeping an eye on you."

"Look all you want, Judge. I was cleared of those charges, and I have nothing to hide." Chance dug his spurs into the flanks of the gray he rode, urging the animal after the other hunters.

* * *

Chance drew his mount to a halt, pulled a handkerchief from his coat, and wiped the beads of sweat from his brow. Judge Turner had been right about one thing—there was no predicting delta weather. A chilly January morning had transformed into a day that rivaled the heat and humidity of spring.

Nor had the promised boar ever materialized. Twice the hounds had bayed and dashed ahead of the hunters on the scent of the prey. The first time, that prey turned out to be a treed raccoon. The second time, the dogs caught and tore apart a rabbit before the riders could reach them.

Chance silently hoped that James Walsh would have the sense to call off the hunt before the dogs led them on a third wild chase. The afternoon still lay ahead, and there was always the possibility of Anne and him slipping off from the others and paying another visit to that old barn.

A blast like thunder tore through the woods!

The gambler's head shot up. Without a cloud in the sky, the sound had not been thunder but the report of a gun—the roar of a shotgun, if he judged correctly. And it came from directly ahead of him. He nudged the gray into an easy gallop.

Around him he heard the shouts of his fellow hunters spread out through the tangled jungle of the wood fringing the bayou. He ignored the crashing sounds as their horses tore through the underbrush, focusing instead on five shaggy pines a half mile in front of him. He was certain the blast had come from beyond those trees.

Reaching the pines, he tugged the gray to a halt. Just on the other side of the trees, the ground opened in a narrow gully five feet deep. James Walsh's black mount lunged in a full run along the bottom of the ditch. No rider sat in the animal's saddle.

"There goes James's horse!" a rider who approached from the gambler's left shouted. "Anyone see James?"

"James? James?" Four more of the mounted hunters pulled up before the ditch. "James? James, where are you, man?"

Chance's stomach lurched as his gaze drifted to the gully's floor. He found the answer to their questioning calls.

"There's no need shouting." The gambler's eyes lifted to the men as ten more horsemen rode up. "He can't hear you anymore."

The men followed the tilt of Chance's head. James Walsh's body lay sprawled in the mud and pooled water at the bottom of the gully, his still smoking double-barreled shotgun beside him.

"My God! His head? Where is his head?" a hunter gasped.

Three of the riders reeled their mounts around, barely nudging their animals beyond the tight line of men who stared below before their stomachs upheaved what remained of their breakfasts.

"It looks like he blew his own head off!" another man said.

Chance looked back at the grisly scene, noticing for the first time the bloody splatter spread across the opposite bank of the gully—the remains of what had once been James Walsh's head. When the gambler's gaze pulled away from the ditch again, he felt eyes peering at him. Those eyes and the granite-set face surrounding them belonged to Judge Harlan Turner. The cold expression that hardened the jurist's features said more than Chance wanted to know. He had no doubt that Turner felt that he was somehow responsible for James's death.

TEN

Detective Jean Defoe was a shock to Chance. After dealing with the average man in blue whom New Orleans called her finest, it took the gambler several minutes to convince himself that the prim-and-proper investigator was not a figment of his imagination.

Defoe had set up office in Graham Walsh's study exactly two hours after James's death was reported to the New Orleans authorities. During those two hours, the small man, standing no more than five foot seven—Chance suspected his actual height was increased by at least an inch, if not more, by the heels of the gleaming black boots he wore—had examined the scene of the hunting tragedy and thoroughly searched the woods around James's body. For the past six hours he had marched the hunt's participants into the study to question them privately. Chance was the last of the male guests to be summoned before the detective.

Like his manner, everything about Jean Defoe was immaculately proper, from the crisp crease in the pants legs of his natty, pin-striped charcoal-hued suit, to his clear, distinctive enunciation of each syllable that passed his lips. The only mildly irritating habit that Chance detected in the man was his occasionally twisting the ends of a thin, waxed mustache so that the ends curled upward toward his nostrils.

And, Chance realized as he evaluated the man who scribbled into a notebook laid out on the desk in front of him, Defoe's right palm kept creeping to the back of his head as though to assure himself that his slicked-down hair remained in its proper place. The mannerism reminded the gambler of a young boy who attempted to smooth an unruly cowlick.

"Harumph." The detective cleared his throat as he looked up from his copious notes. "You admit that you were the first to find James Walsh's body, is that correct?"

Defoe's gentle voice, almost effeminate in its softness, was deceptive, Chance recognized. It took but one glance at the man's dark eyes to catch a glimmering of the investigator's intelligence. Defoe was alert, his mind ready to alight on a single alteration in the gambler's original recounting. The detective was definitely not a man to underestimate.

"I believe that I've said this three times before." Chance kept his impatience in check. "I was the first to *see* James's body. Myself and several others in the hunting party arrived at the gully at practically the same moment."

"Yes." Defoe nodded and glanced back to his notes. "Did you notice anyone or thing at the scene when you rode up?"

"Nothing but James's horse running away," the gambler replied. "But then I had no reason to be looking for anything out of the ordinary."

"No, no, you didn't," the detective agreed. "However, it never hurts to ask if anyone noticed anything unusual at an accident scene—especially in light of the strange threat made on the Walsh family last night."

Chance couldn't contradict that. After last night, murder had been the first thing that flashed into his mind when he had seen James's body sprawled in the mud at the bottom of the gully. "Then you feel that James's death was an accident?"

Detective Defoe leaned back into a massive chair that nearly swallowed his small form. He steepled his fingers, pursed his lips, and nodded. "I have found no evidence to indicate that there was foul play involved, Mr. Sharpe. Unless one gives credence to supernatural beings with powers to carry out threats from beyond the grave, there is no other conclusion to reach except that James Walsh died when his horse threw him and he was caught in the blast of his own shotgun's misfire."

"I don't believe in ghosts or phantoms, Detective," Chance said. "But I assure you that I, along with every other guest in the dining room last night, saw someone—or some*thing*—threaten Graham Walsh and his family."

Defoe leaned forward, his dark eyes seeming to pierce the gambler. "Then you have reason to believe that things are other than they appear?"

"No evidence, if that's what you're after." Chance met the policeman's unblinking gaze. "But I think that if I were in your position, I'd feel the situation was slightly out of kilter to discover a man with his head blown away only a few hours after someone threatened to kill every member of his family."

Chance also recounted the attacks on Anne and Warren, and the poison-dipped wooden blades their assailants carried. Defoe listened, flipped back through several pages of his notebook, and finally glanced at the gambler again.

"Both Miss Anne Walsh and her brother Warren described these incidents to me," the detective said. "In both of their accounts, you were named as their rescuer."

Something in Defoe's tone caught in Chance's mind. His eyes narrowed for an instant. "Are you implying that I was somehow behind those attacks?"

The detective smiled, the curled ends of his mustache almost touching his nose. "I was merely illustrating a point concerning coincidence, Mr. Sharpe. Others might have drawn false conclusions concerning your participation in the two attacks simply from a matter of coincidence. But *a man in my position*, who is a trained and experienced sleuth, would never jump to such conclusions without specific evidence."

The words were right, but somehow Chance couldn't quite accept the detective's sincerity. "Then, your official conclusion is that James Walsh died in a freak hunting accident?"

Defoe nodded as though displaying the patience of Job. "Which is exactly what I intend to tell the surviving members of the family, if you will be so kind as to ask them to join me here as soon as you leave, Mr. Sharpe."

If Chance had ever heard a dismissal, that was one. The gambler rose from his chair and left the den to find Anne and tell her that the detective wanted to speak with the members of her family.

"It doesn't make sense." Anne's arm slid across the gambler's chest to cling closely to the warmth of his body. "James had never been thrown by a horse once in his life."

Chance lightly stroked a palm over the silky strands of her hair as he pressed his lips to the top of her head. Anne had crept into his bed for comfort this night, not for lovemaking. His own left arm tightened around her slender waist, drawing her close.

"Even with the use of only one arm, James had a special way with horses," Anne continued. "I can't believe that he took a spill and his shotgun went off, accidentally killing him. I can't!''

The gambler said nothing, but held her even closer. He understood her doubts, had shared them earlier. However, the more he thought about it, the more sense Defoe made. There had been no evidence of foul play around the ditch. Nor had a wooden knife been involved. He simply couldn't see a connection between the attacks on Anne and Warren and James's death.

Nestled in the hollow of his shoulder, Anne's diminutive body shuddered repeatedly. He felt the warmth of her tears trickle against his skin. All he could do was kiss her again and wrap his right arm about her trembling body. The truth was, no matter how expert a rider a man was, sooner or later he was bound to be tossed from a mount. The odds of that happening to a man with one good arm were increased greatly.

''The other thing I don't understand is why did Mother have to be so civil to that weasely little policeman? Why did she ask him to spend the night?'' Bitterness seeped through Anne's tears. ''He wouldn't even consider the possibility that James had been murdered!''

''Your mother is a lady,'' Chance replied softly. ''The lateness of the hour dictated that she offer Detective Defoe a room for the night.''

''You're right, of course,'' Anne eventually answered. ''I still don't like him being around.''

''Shhhh,'' the gambler hushed her. ''It's too late to worry about it now. Why don't you see if you can sleep? A few hours' rest will do you good.''

''I don't feel sleepy,'' she protested.

However, within mere minutes physical and emotional exhaustion won out. Anne drifted into a gentle sleep.

ELEVEN

Chance woke Anne as the dim glow of the new day began to filter through the heavy gray rain clouds that blanketed the Louisiana sky. She kissed him, slipped into her robe, and returned to her own room.

Glancing at the rumpled bed sheets, the gambler considered returning to sleep, then discarded the idea. There was nothing lonelier than an empty bed that had held a woman's warmth but moments ago. Instead, he located his coat neatly placed over the back of a chair, fumbled through the pockets until he found a cigar, and lit it. He settled into a chair he placed beside a window, and stared outside.

The dreary grayness that hung in the air dampened the spirits, as though constantly reminding him of the sorrow that had entered this house. *It'll rain during the funeral,* he thought as his eyes rolled to the building clouds. Now that Defoe had officially pronounced James Walsh's death an accident, his body would be hastily interred. Even during the winter, delta temperatures demanded prompt attention to the last rites of departed loved ones.

When the slender, black saber had burned to a stub, he stuffed out the butt in an ashtray. A chilly pitcher of water, a bar of soap, and a towel set beside a washbasin atop a small table in one corner of the room provided the gambler with an eye-opening, gooseflesh-rippling bath and shave. He then dressed in black suit and tie before walking downstairs.

The few guests who had awakened early gathered in the dining room where they partook of chicory-laced coffee and hot doughnuts. Few spoke, but all constantly glanced at one another. Distress was evident in their eyes and in the drawn expressions that tautened their faces. Each had come for a weekend of gaiety and now found himself in the middle of a family's personal tragedy. All wished to be elsewhere, but etiquette demanded that they remain until a dead son had been laid to rest.

The turn of heads within the room drew Chance's attention to the dining room's entrance. Elouise, with Anne a few steps behind her older sister, crossed the threshold. Both women were dressed in black.

"Friends . . . " Elouise began, then paused to draw a steadying breath and started over. "Friends, my parents asked me to apologize for their tardiness this morning. Both Father and Mother will be down to join you shortly."

Chance took a step toward Anne and abruptly halted. A woman's scream echoed through the mansion. Without hesitation, the gambler darted from the dining room.

"It's Missus Walsh!" a black maid wailed from the top of the stairway, her arms waving wildly in the air. "Sweet Jesus! Oh, sweet Jesus!"

"Alita!" Elouise reached Chance's side and shouted up to the hysterical woman. "Alita, what is wrong?"

"It's . . . it's Missus Walsh," the maid barely managed to answer. "She . . . she done . . . taken the fallin' sickness!"

At Elouise's heels and with the rest of the household following, Chance moved up the stairs two at a time and then rushed down a wide walnut-paneled hallway toward an open bedroom door. From a room at the far end of the hall, Graham Walsh hastened to his wife's bedroom.

"Rachael!" The name tore from Graham's lips as a wail of pain and agony when he reached the open door. "No! God, no! Not Rachael!"

Inside, Rachael Walsh lay crumpled on the floor in front of her delicately carved vanity. The soft folds of the diaphanous pink dressing gown she wore were undisturbed by the rise and fall of her breast.

"She was sitting there abrushin' her hair," the maid Alita said somewhere behind the gambler. "I was layin' out her black dress like she told me when she suddenly tumbled over and fell to the floor. I called to her, but she didn't answer me. It didn't do no good to shake her, either."

"Let me through, please!" Detective Jean Defoe demanded. Upon entering the bedroom, the slight-built policeman straightened his suit, then crossed to the fallen woman. He touched a finger to her neck before placing an ear against her chest. Finally he lifted a mirror from the dressing table and held it above her lips. When he turned to the door, he simply said, "I'm afraid Mrs. Walsh is dead."

"Noooo!" Another anguished cry tore from Graham Walsh's lips. "It's the curse! God help us all! It's the curse!"

Shoving those in his path aside, the massively built man fought his way free of the guests crowded around him. He then ran down the hall into his own room, slamming the door behind him.

"Everyone"—Defoe's tone demanded attention—"please return downstairs. I must examine this room and the body alone."

*   *   *

When the short detective called the Walsh family upstairs an hour later, Chance accompanied the brother and sisters at Anne's request. Even if he had wanted to remain behind, he doubted that he could have broken the tight grip that Anne held on his hand.

However, his appearance did lift one of Defoe's eyebrows in question. "I didn't realize you had become a member of the Walsh family, Mr. Sharpe."

"I asked him to come," Anne said before Chance could reply to the policeman.

Defoe's thin-lipped mouth twisted in disgust, but he made no further reference to the gambler's presence. Instead, he looked at Elouise and said, "I have attempted to talk with your father, but he refuses to admit me to his room. Will you assist me? I can find nothing that hints that your mother died of anything more than natural causes—perhaps the distress of her son's death. However, your father's reaction to her death indicates that his opinion may differ. I must question him."

Chance added another item to the detective's list of irritating habits—Defoe never used a single word when he could stretch it to ten.

"Are you certain this is necessary?" Elouise made no attempt to hide her impatience with the officer.

"Not only is it necessary, but absolutely essential, if I am to gather all the facts concerning your mother's untimely demise," the detective answered. "I would not intrude on you or your family under these circumstances if it were not."

Elouise drew a heavy breath and nodded wearily. She then turned and strode to the door of her father's bedroom. After rapping on the door, she spoke in an indiscernibly soft voice for several minutes before returning to the detective. "He says that he'll talk with you, but only if all of us are present in the room—including Mr. Sharpe.''

Again Defoe's thin lips curled with disgust, but he acquiesced to the elder Walsh's demands and waved an arm for Elouise to lead the way.

A shuffle of feet came from behind the bedroom door; metallic clicks at the lock slid from its niche; then another hasty scurry of retreating feet. Elouise grasped the door's handle and pushed in. An effluvium of stale tobacco smoke and bourbon rushed from the room.

"Inside, all of you," Graham called out. "Close and lock that door behind you."

Chance was last to enter the room. He did as Graham requested. When he turned, he found the head of the Walsh family seated in an overstuffed chair on the opposite side of the large bedroom. In his hand was an old Navy Colt that had been modified to accept cartridges in its cylinder. He lifted the revolver and pointed it directly at Defoe.

However, when he spoke it was to all his visitors. "If you wish to sit, please use the side of the bed. If you want to stand, stay right where you are. I don't want anyone coming closer."

"Father," Elouise pleaded, "we're your family."

"I have no family, except the walking dead," Graham answered. "Don't any of you understand that? You're all marked to die—all because of me."

Chance edged to the left for an unobstructed view of the man. The wild light in Graham's eyes and his rock-steady grip on the Colt were not to be argued with—nor were the shotgun and rifle that stood leaning against the left side of his chair. Apparently Elouise noticed the unmistakable signs of madness in her father's face and pressed him no further.

"Cursed!" Graham's left hand stretched out and lifted a glass of bourbon from a round table positioned just beyond the rifle and shotgun. He took a long drink. "You saw that damned Indian demon; you heard him. He marked us all for the grave. Ask Rachael and James about his power, if you don't believe me."

"Mr. Walsh, both your wife and son are dead," Detective Defoe said in that soft voice of his. "They can't tell us anything. However, you can—"

"I didn't believe in the curse." Graham ignored the police officer. "Hell, I'd all but forgotten about it until you were attacked in Saint Louis, Anne." His eyes alighted on his youngest daughter and then drifted to Warren. "Still wasn't certain until you were jumped on the *Wild Card*, Warren. Then I knew it wasn't just a coincidence. Nobody but those bloody heathens use wooden knives drenched in poison."

"Heathens?" Chance asked.

"The devils who spat their curse in my face." Graham didn't glance at the gambler, but sucked down another swallow of bourbon. "Damned Indians. We hadn't planned to kill anyone. What we were after was slaves. Only, there weren't any."

"Father, what are you talking about?" Warren took a step forward, and Graham's pistol swung to cover his sole living son. The youngest Walsh halted immediately. "What Indians are you talking about?"

"Those in South America," Graham answered. "They aren't like the Comanche or Sioux; they're children of the Devil himself."

Graham paused to fortify himself with another slug of alcohol. "James had just been born when I signed up to ship out on the *Southern Cross*. She was a sleek, pretty ship bound for Brazil to fill her holds with coffee. I was young, the pay was good, and I was ready to make my fortune."

The elder Walsh recounted how the *Southern Cross* made her Brazilian port, but only half the expected cargo awaited the sailing ship. "The captain wasn't a man to return to New Orleans with half his hold empty: there was no profit to be made in that. The evening after we had laid aboard all the coffee, he gathered the crew together and told us that there was quick gold to be made and he was willing to share the unexpected windfall with every man sailing under him."

That windfall was escaped slaves, Graham explained. The slaves—two hundred men, women, and children—had taken over an abandoned Indian village a hundred miles up the coast. The captain assured his men that there was room enough for all two hundred in the *Southern Cross*'s hold.

"So we set sail and crept northward, following the coast until we sighted the village's camp fires one night," Graham said. "We weighed anchor."

Armed with rifle, pistol, or knife, every man aboard the vessel took part in the night raid. Silently they slipped from their ship into longboats and rowed to shore.

"We surrounded the village, and at the captain's signal, we attacked. Indians rather than blacks came rushing at us out of those grass huts—and we cut them down one after another, man, woman, or child," Graham said. "We thought that they were protecting the runaway slaves. It wasn't until most of the village lay dead on the ground that we realized that there weren't any slaves, only those painted heathens. With our guns still blazing, we began our retreat."

He paused for another deep drink of bourbon. "That's when their medicine man stepped from a hut and stood among the dead. He wailed and screamed in his devil's tongue, and then in the plainest Spanish he turned to us. His eyes glowed demon red when he spat at us and proclaimed that we were all cursed—that the ghosts of his slain village would seek us out and destroy us and all who carried our blood."

Graham said one of the crewmen fired at the medicine man, but missed. The Indian darted into the jungle's darkness.

"Not one of us suffered a scratch, nor did we do more than laugh at the curse as we set sail for home," he continued the grisly tale. "It was off the coast of northern Mexico that the storm hit. Almost out of nowhere it swept down on the *Southern Cross,* snapping our masts like they were dry twigs. There was nothing we could do except pray. And that didn't help. The storm blew us straight onto a rocky coast. The *Southern Cross* shattered. I'm still not certain how I lived through the sinking, but I did—I was the only one who did. All the rest of the crew went down with the ship."

It was Anne who spoke when her father paused again. "But that was years ago, almost another lifetime. Surely you can't still believe in the curse."

"I can and do!" Graham's voice tinged with anger. "No one else uses damned wooden blades like those. And it was that medicine man who appeared in the storm the other night—him or his ghost. I've eluded him all these years; now he's found me again and there's no escape!"

"Father," Elouise began, "there's no curse. It's only superstitious nonsense. You can't—"

"Nonsense!" Graham cocked the Colt and pointed its long muzzle at his oldest daughter. "All of you out of here. I tried to tell you the truth, and you call it nonsense. Now get out!"

No one argued; against that Colt there could be only one winner.

As Chance stepped back into the hall, closing the bedroom behind him, he realized that Graham Walsh had spoken the truth—at least for himself—when he had said that there was no escape. For the head of the Walsh family, past sins and guilts had already trapped him in a cage of insanity.

TWELVE

Rachael Walsh and her son James were interred in a family mausoleum built near the stand of pines that Chance and Anne had ridden through on Friday afternoon. The parish priest kept his words concise and short, in deference to the large crowd attending the funeral and the steady rain that beat down upon umbrellas and heads.

Following the service, the guests once more paid their sympathies to the two sisters and brother—Graham Walsh remained locked in his bedroom with his bourbon and guns to ward off ghosts from his past—and then departed to return to New Orleans and the world of the living. By the time Homer Lincoln pulled his hack to a halt before the Walsh mansion, even Detective Jean Defoe had mounted and ridden back to the city—but not before poking around the plantation in the rain for at least two hours and never offering an explanation of his activities.

Chance had packed his bags, and was halfway down the stairway with them when Anne appeared, pleading with him to stay at least one more night. "The house is too empty without Mother and James. I need you here, Chance."

He agreed, and directed the cabbie back to New Orleans with directions to return for him the next afternoon. Homer offered no complaints about the long drive, but merely tipped a rain-drenched silk top hat sporting an orange tulip and clucked Bad Bad forward.

Chance then joined Anne and her brother and sister in a small sitting room where the three watched the falling rain trickle down the windows and reminisced about their lost loved ones until the butler announced that dinner was served.

Other than Elouise's ordering a tray to be taken up to her father, none of the three siblings spoke, nor could Chance offer a topic of conversation that would lighten their sorrow. Only Anne's hand, which reached out and repeatedly squeezed his during the meal, provided any assurance that he was indeed wanted within the house.

As the servants cleared the table, Elouise and Anne announced that they both intended to retire early, leaving Warren and the gambler staring at each other when the two women climbed the stairs to the mansion's second floor.

"I don't think I can face bed at the moment," Warren said. "I'm still awake, and there are too many memories crowding my head. Can I interest you in a game of billiards? If not, perhaps a drink—anything to help take my mind off all that has happened."

"You can interest me in both," Chance answered.

Warren smiled, obviously relieved by the gambler's company. He motioned Chance from the dining room, down a long hall to a room with a billiard table set at its center. "There are an assortment of liquors in the cabinet. Please help yourself."

Chance opened the cabinet and located a bottle of Kentucky bourbon while Warren selected a cue from a rack on the wall. "What are you drinking?"

The young man glanced up from the balls he arranged on the table and shook his head. "It might sound a bit foolish, but I promised Mother that I wouldn't partake of alcoholic beverages until I was twenty-one.''

The gambler didn't laugh, but said, ''Not a bad promise to keep for the rest of your life. Too many men let alcohol use them rather than their using it.''

When Chance selected a cue stick and turned back to the table, he found Warren by a window staring into the night. ''Is there anything you'd like to talk about, Warren?''

''I'm not certain that I can put it into words,'' he replied without glancing away from the window and the rain outside.

''That's easy enough to understand. This family and your life have been struck by an emotional earthquake.''

''But it's more than just losing Mother and James.'' Warren faced the older man. ''It's father and all he said this morning.''

''And what he's become?'' Chance answered.

The younger man nodded. ''He was always the strong one—the granite foundation on which this family rested. Now . . . and now I'm not certain what he's become.''

''There are doctors who can help,'' Chance suggested. ''He won't do himself any good locked away in his bedroom with a small arsenal at his fingertips.''

''I've thought of that,'' Warren said as he stared out the window once more. ''But have you ever seen an insane asylum, Chance? We treat our hounds better than the patients in those places.''

''I didn't mention an asylum,'' the gambler replied as he placed his cue atop the untouched table. ''I said a doctor, one that could treat your father here in his own home. I have a friend, Philip Duwayne, who I could ask to help locate the right physician, if you wish.''

"I would be . . ." Warren's words trailed off, and his knuckles turned white beneath his grip on the cue stick he still held. "Chance! Someone's outside! I just saw him dart toward the bayou!"

"What?" Chance crossed to Warren's side and cupped a hand against a windowpane to shut out the room's reflected light; he peered outside. "Where?"

"There by that twin-trunked cypress," Warren said with a tilt of his head to the left. "For an instant, he looked like Father's Indian visitor Friday night."

Chance saw a vague shadow clinging to the double-trunked tree—and it *did* appear to be the long-haired apparition. Only this was no ghostly visitor; it was a half-naked man huddled in the cold rain.

"I'm going after him," Warren said, spinning away from the window and running toward the door of the billiard room. "Maybe he can give me the answers I'm looking for!"

"Warren, wait!" Chance called after the young man. Warren didn't hesitate, but darted down the long hall, abruptly turning toward the kitchen and the house's rear exit. "Damn!"

The gambler pressed a palm against his stomach, feeling the comforting bulk of his belly-gun and the derringer in his vest pocket. He then ran after Warren, finding the young man standing in the rain just outside the back door.

"There he goes!" Warren jabbed a pointing finger toward the bayou. There was no doubt about the shadow's being a man now. He bolted from the twin-boled cypress and shot into the dense underbrush.

"He's getting away. Come on, we can catch him," Warren shouted to his companion as he sprinted toward the bayou.

Lightning flashed overhead when the two men pushed through the underbrush and came upon a narrow path that led deeper into the swamp. Warren again pointed, his finger stabbing in the direction the path led. "He had to go that way. If he went straight, he'd end up bogged down in the bayou. He had to take the path!"

Before Chance could suggest that they both return to the house, Warren was running again. With another curse, the gambler followed the young man.

A half-mile later, Warren stumbled to a halt. His head twisted from side to side as he scanned the jungle of vegetation in the white light that flared from overhead. He opened his mouth and his lips moved, but his words were drowned by the rolling crash of thunder.

"What?" Chance shouted above the deafening explosion of the elements.

"I think I saw him over there," Warren repeated and motioned to the left. "If we hurry, we can get him."

"Warren, I don't see anything." Chance wiped away the rivulets of water that ran from his forehead into his eyes and stared in the direction the young man motioned. He then searched the area around them. "Are you certain you saw something? My bet is that he kept to the path."

The gambler turned back to Warren. The young man wasn't there! "Stupid, damned stupid, Warren."

Nor could he find any trace of his companion. Spitting out a string of curses, he left the path, pushing into the tangled underbrush in the direction where Warren had sighted the fleeing man.

"Warren! Warren!" Chance shouted as he ran after the young man. "Warren! Warren!"

Only the pounding rain and the thunder answered him.

THIRTEEN

"This is where you lost Warren Walsh last night?" Detective Jean Defoe glanced at the muddy path and then at Chance. "Are you certain?"

"No, I'm not certain," the gambler replied.

"Didn't you note some landmark, such as that log over there?" Defoe pointed to a fallen cypress hardly noticeable beneath a coat of lush moss.

"No, I didn't note a landmark," Chance answered, barely able to contain his exasperation with the prim-and-proper police officer. "It was raining—storming—last night; I couldn't see five feet ahead of me, let alone get a clear view of this terrain. Besides, I didn't think that I'd need a landmark when I went after Warren. I thought he was only a short distance ahead of me. I didn't realize that I'd lost him."

"Then why did you pick this particular spot, Mr. Sharpe, if you are so uncertain about where you departed from the path last night?"

Defoe was relentless with his verbose questions. Chance began to wonder why he had sent for the authorities in the first place. In truth, he knew: after Warren hadn't returned to the mansion by dawn, he realized that he required assistance in searching the bayou for the young man and had sent a servant into New Orleans to inform the police of what had happened.

However, he hadn't expected Defoe to respond to his call for help—Defoe and five blue-uniformed policemen.

Chance pointed down. "See those weeds? They've been trampled. Notice the brambles there? They've been broken. My guess is that Warren and I did that last night when we left the path."

"And you could not have searched without the police's aid?" the short detective asked.

"I already told you that I tried searching and almost got myself lost again," Chance answered, sensing that Defoe wasn't believing a word he said.

The officer fiddled with the ends of his mustache for several moments while he stared at the trampled vegetation. Finally he glanced at the five men behind them on the path and said, "Very well, we shall begin our search at this point. You men spread out and move into the bayou. Call out if you notice anything I should see."

Defoe stayed by the gambler's side as they moved from the path. From the corner of an eye, Chance saw an expression of disdain darken the investigator's face when he glanced down at his boots and pant cuffs. The gambler smiled. Both were soaking wet and splattered with dark mud.

"Excuse me if I repeat myself, but I am attempting to arrange the events of the previous night in their correct order in my mind," the detective said. "It was Warren Walsh who noticed this strange man, was it not?"

For the fifth time since Defoe's arrival at the plantation, Chance recounted everything that had occurred after Anne and Elouise retired for the night. The detective listened while patting his pomade-slicked hair.

"This is as far as I went earlier," Chance said, pointing to a copse of five pines. "I remember those trees."

"You remember those trees, yet you can recall no landmark from last night?"

"It was dark and storming last night, remember, Defoe?"

"Yes," the man answered with a nod that said he completely missed or ignored the sarcasm in the gambler's tone. "I do seem to remember you mentioning something about thunder and lightning. Shall we press on and see what lies ahead?"

"After you, Detective." Chance waved an arm, signaling the policeman to lead the way. "You are 'the trained and experienced sleuth,' after all."

"Quite so," Defoe replied, apparently not recognizing that the gambler threw his own words back in his face.

Chance's mouth twisted in disgust as he watched the officer plod deeper into the bayou's jungle of vegetation. Perhaps he had overestimated the detective yesterday. Today Defoe appeared to be the incompetent dolt the gambler had come to associate with New Orleans's postwar police force.

"It seems that you didn't push your search far enough earlier, Mr. Sharpe." The detective halted and pointed toward a cypress fifty feet ahead.

Chance's stomach churned when he located what had caught Defoe's eye—Warren Walsh. The young man lay on his back in the mud with a fire-charred branch protruding from the center of his chest.

"A death as grotesque and horrible as the one his older brother suffered, wouldn't you say, Mr. Sharpe?" Defoe produced a silver whistle from a coat pocket and blew shrilly on it to summon the other policemen to him. He then walked beside the dead man and stared down at the lifeless body. "Perhaps even a more cruel death. Warren Walsh was certain to have known what was happening to him before life fled his body."

Chance followed the detective's gaze upward to the heights of the towering cypress. A blackened, charred scar marred the trunk among the lofty branches.

"What is it, Detective?" one of the policemen asked as the five answered the whistle. In the next moment, the man's face went ashen when his gaze alighted on the impaled corpse of Warren Walsh. "My God! How did that happen?"

As though completely removed from the situation, Defoe replied, "It would appear that this tree was struck by lightning during last night's storm, officer. Fate placed the unfortunate Mr. Walsh beneath this limb as it fell to earth."

"And it's skewered him like a pig on a spit!" another of the policemen added.

"A melodramatic description, but an accurate one," the detective said with a tilt of his head. "There's nothing else I need to see here. You men may carry the body back to the Walsh home whenever you're ready."

Defoe started back over the path that had led them to the dead man, then glanced back at Chance. "Mr. Sharpe, if you'll be so kind as to accompany me, there are several things I would like to discuss with you."

Although Detective Defoe had yet to come right out and say it, Chance knew exactly what the verbose policeman was getting at halfway back to the Walsh mansion. "Are you accusing me of murdering Rachael Walsh and her two sons?"

"You've had a colorful career since your release from the army, Mr. Sharpe. Certain aspects of it have been publicized highly," the officer said.

"Why don't you just come out and say that Judge Turner has bent your ear, Defoe?" Chance imagined the old jurist dragging the policeman aside and conveying his suspicions.

"I must admit that I have been aware of Chance Sharpe for some time. Since you won a court case against an attorney named Rapper, as a matter of fact."

Chance cursed silently to himself. That attorney had stolen the *Wild Card* by manipulating back-tax notices. A slightly rigged horse race and some fancy legal maneuvering by Philip Duwayne had won the riverboat back.

"However, I had never considered that you were anything more than a successful confidence man until Judge Turner and I recently had a discussion concerning the murder of Wilson Morehead."

"I was cleared of those charges in Turner's own courtroom," Chance replied, doing his damnedest to keep his temper under tight reins.

"Under less than satisfying circumstances, to my way of thinking," Defoe said.

Chance held his tongue as they entered the house through the kitchen door. He had said more to the detective than he wanted and wouldn't speak another word until he met with Philip for advice.

Reaching the hallway, Defoe turned to the gambler and said, "I have no evidence and I am making no charges, Mr. Sharpe, but rest assured that I am on to you. I don't know how or why you are killing off the members of the Walsh family, but I intend to find out. And when I do, you will swing from a hangman's rope for your crimes. I promise you that!"

FOURTEEN

Chance held his temper in check . . . barely. This pompous little popinjay was no different from any policeman the gambler had ever met. Detective Jean Defoe found himself with three deaths on his hands and was grasping at straws to explain them. The trouble was, the straw he clutched the tightest was one named Chance Sharpe!

Although rage and frustration seethed within the gambler's breast, he maintained a cool outward appearance, nor did anger creep into his voice. "You're trying to pull rabbits out of thin air, Defoe, and you damned well know it. There's no evidence that indicates I had anything to do with the deaths, and you yourself have ruled no foul play in all three incidents."

A smug smile stretched the policeman's thin lips. "Your mistake is a preponderance of coincidences, Sharpe—enough that a jury might consider them circumstantial evidence," Defoe replied with equal coolness. "As I said, I have no hard evidence to connect you with the deaths, nor do I even have proof that the deaths were more than they seem. *But*, the pattern to your method is more than apparent."

"Pattern to my method?" Chance could not contain his exasperation. "What in hell are you talking about?"

"It began with the attacks on Anne and Warren Walsh—the use of those poisoned wooden knives. Attacks that you arranged so that you might prove to be the noble rescuer and ingratiate yourself with Graham and Rachael Walsh and garner an invitation into their home," Defoe said, his dark eyes transforming to icy orbs as he stared at the gambler.

"Defoe, *I* nearly died when one of those knives nicked the back of my hand. You're not making sense." Disgust replaced the exasperation in Chance's voice.

"A mistake on your part, Sharpe, which almost ruined your scheme to destroy the Walsh family," the detective continued. "Coincidences, Sharpe. The coincidences began to pile one atop the other once you arrived here. First there was the well-staged ghostly visitor at Friday's dinner and nothing to link you to that apparition. However, you slipped the next morning when you killed James Walsh. You were the first to arrive at the scene of his death, according to the other guests—perhaps you arrived before James himself and arranged his riding accident?"

Chance merely shook his head in disbelief: words were no good with the detective.

"And you were the first to arrive at Rachael Walsh's room yesterday when she collapsed—yet another coincidence, Sharpe," Defoe verbally checked off the list he had compiled against the gambler. "Last night you went too far. You were the only one with Warren Walsh when he supposedly disappeared in the bayou."

Chance opened his mouth to answer the policeman's ludicrous accusations, then swallowed his words. Defoe was trying to dig a trap beneath him, and anything that he said would be twisted by the detective. He had to talk with Philip Duwayne.

"Then you do not deny the scenario that I've described?" Defoe curled the ends of his waxed mustache.

"Defoe . . ." Chance began.

A woman's scream shattered the gambler's train of thought. Chance's head snapped around as another high-pitched cry of terror tore through the mansion. "Anne!"

He darted from the kitchen right behind the small detective. Nor did he overtake the surprisingly spry man as they bounded up the stairway to the home's second floor. Another scream hastened them down the walnut-paneled hall to the open door to Elouise's bedroom. The woman huddled against a wall; her horror-widened eyes stared at the windows.

"The ghost!" she shouted when the two men rushed into the bedroom. "It was there—glaring at me through the windows. I saw the ghost!"

Defoe crossed the room in the blink of an eye. A self-pleased grin split his face when he glanced back at the gambler. "You and your accomplice have overplayed your hands, Sharpe! If I am swift of foot, both of you shall be locked behind bars by tonight!"

With that, the detective darted from the room. Chance's gaze shot out the window to the well-manicured lawn below. The light of day left no doubt as to the reality of what Elouise had seen. A small, wiry, cinnamon-skinned Indian—naked except for a leather breechclout—ran at full speed toward the woods fringing the bayou. The gambler pivoted and raced from the bedroom after Defoe.

A quarter of a mile along the swamp path, Chance caught up with the detective, who stood beside the five uniformed officers carrying Warren Walsh's body.

"Small and dark, yes, sir," one of the policeman said and pointed toward the mansion. "He came flying around that turn like the very Devil was on his heels— nearly ran smack-dab over us!''

"And not one of you illustrious gentlemen attempted to stop him?'' Disbelief filled Defoe's voice.

"Wasn't time,'' another of the officers answered. "He shot by us and hightailed it down the path before we knew what was happening.''

The detective mumbled something, shook his head in obvious disgust, and started down the path as fast as his short legs could carry him. Chance ran right beside him.

"Coming along to make certain that I don't apprehend your cohort?'' Defoe shot a glance at the gambler.

"To make sure that you *do* get him! He's the only way that I'll get you off my back, Defoe.'' Chance grinned at the small policeman, then glanced down at the path. The bare feet of the man they chased left an easy trail in the mud. "Stay off the path or you'll destroy his trail!''

Defoe immediately responded by scooting to one side of the path, while the gambler's strides carried him along the other. It didn't help; a half-mile farther into the bayou, the footprints suddenly disappeared. The two men stumbled to a halt, gasping to catch their breaths.

"It appears that your ghost has conveniently vanished into nothingness, Sharpe.'' The detective's head swung from side to side, searching the underbrush.

Chance scanned the limbs of the trees above and found the same thing as Defoe—nothing. "He might have realized he was leaving a trail and started moving through the grass just as we did.''

"Perhaps,'' the investigator answered with a dubiously arched eyebrow when he started along the bayou path once again at a slower pace.

Here and there in the grass and weeds Chance thought he saw spots that might have been made by a man's foot. However, he couldn't be certain. The recent storms had been hard; both wind and rain had beaten down the vegetation, leaving it flat against the ground in the area along the path.

"You have won this round, Sharpe." Defoe halted, and dabbed a handkerchief at the beads of sweat dotting his forehead. "For now, I'll admit defeat. But I warn you, I haven't given up. I intend to uncover the methods you employed in committing these gruesome atrocities."

"Give up, Defoe." Chance kept plodding down the path. "We've only come a mile and a half or so. I'd like to know exactly where this leads. I'll tell you what I find when I get back."

The gambler heard the policeman mumble something under his breath, then a series of soggy footsteps as Defoe caught up with him.

"This performance will not deter me, Sharpe," the detective said, casting a suspicious glance at Chance. "I am fully aware of your motives."

"You know, Defoe, I think that I like you better, the shorter your wind gets." Chance returned the detective's glance. "It whittles your sentences down by about three-fourths. By the way, your mustache is starting to droop."

While Defoe fiddled with the upturned ends of his mustache, the gambler increased the tempo of his long strides, amusing himself with the huffing and wheezing that came from the small detective while he tried to keep up with the larger man. After another quarter of a mile, the gambler slowed to a more leisurely pace. The last thing he wanted was for Defoe to suffer a heart attack—and have the New Orleans police accusing him of four murders. Three was enough by far!

"We're coming out of the bayou." An expression of relief washed over the detective's strained face as he pointed ahead.

Chance looked up to find that the path and the woods abruptly ended, and a close-cropped field of winter brown grass stretched before them for another quarter of a mile. The field held no interest for the gambler. His attention centered on a white house with a dark shingled roof that sat in the middle of the field.

"I didn't realize the Walshes had neighbors so close." Defoe started toward the house.

Chance didn't answer. In his mind he ran over the guests to which he had been introduced on his first night in the mansion. He vaguely recalled Anne's labeling one of the guests a neighbor, but he couldn't remember a name or a face.

In comparison to the Walsh mansion, this one-story structure appeared to be no more than a modest country home. In actuality its size equaled the townhouses constructed in New Orleans by plantation owners prior to the outbreak of the Civil War. A large family could occupy such a house and still have room for several visitors without the dogs and cats getting underfoot.

A man dressed in a white suit that was more appropriate for the heat of spring and summer than for mid-January—in spite of the unseasonably warm day—got up from a white swing hung from a porch that ran along the full length of the house. He walked to the porch stairs, leaned against a support column, and waved a welcome to the two men.

"Good day, gentlemen." The tall, handsome, dark-haired man flashed a pleasing smile as the two approached. "You gave me quite a start there for a moment when I saw you coming out of the bayou." The man paused, and his eyes narrowed for a moment, and then widened in recognition. "Mr. Sharpe's the name, if my memory serves me correctly, isn't it? You were one of the guests at the Walsh estate last weekend.''

"Captain Balinger.'' Chance remembered the man's name the instant he got a clear view of his face. He shook Michael Balinger's proffered hand and then introduced Detective Defoe.

"Won't you two come inside and allow me to pour you a drink? Y'all both look as though you could use a spot of refreshment. This humidity can drain a man.'' Balinger walked to his front door, opened it, and waved an arm, signaling his visitors inside.

"Mr. Balinger, I'm afraid that we don't have—''

Chance cut the detective off. "Refreshment, especially if it happens to look, smell, and taste like bourbon, would be greatly appreciated.''

"Straight, or with a drop of branch water?'' Balinger asked as he led the two into a large study with walls sporting hunting trophies and a large array of weapons hung in neat rows.

"Straight.'' Chance's gaze roved over the assorted rifles, shotguns, pistols, swords, and knives while Balinger opened a liquor cabinet and poured three bourbons. "An impressive collection, Mr. Balinger. Very impressive.''

"Michael,'' the man corrected as he handed Chance and Defoe their drinks. "I accumulated the majority of them during my years at sea. I'm a bit embarrassed to admit it, but these indicate my tendency to be a pack rat rather than having any practical value for me. Most of these weapons have never been used. I'm afraid that I've never been much of a hunter or even that good of a shot.''

Chance didn't attempt to hide his surprise. "I would have thought that a man who surrounded himself with such an arsenal would be the type to spend his every free minute hunting game of some sort.''

Balinger shrugged and smiled meekly. "Actually my collection began when two English gentlemen presented me with those two shotguns by the door as a token of their gratitude for bringing them through a particularly fierce storm off the coast of Africa. In fact, half the items you see were given to me by passengers and clients. The others I purchased at different ports because I found their workmanship intriguing or their design unusual."

Chance studied the man over the rim of his glass as he tasted the bourbon and found it to his liking. There was something unsettling about Balinger's meek smile. Perhaps it was *too* meek, or maybe it was discordant with the spark in his dark eyes when he looked at the displayed weapons. The gambler wasn't sure.

"I'm certain that the history of each of these magnificent pieces is most interesting, Mr. Balinger, but this is not the appropriate time to discuss them," Defoe spoke up, placing his bourbon aside without touching it.

Chance grimaced; the verbosity of that single sentence said that the detective had regained his wind.

"Today Warren Walsh was found dead in the bayou between your home and the Walsh estate," Defoe said. "Within the past hour Miss Elouise Walsh was frightened by an intruder peering into her second-floor window."

"What?" Balinger's eyes shifted between the gambler and the detective. "Warren is dead? What happened?"

Defoe explained how the young man was found. Balinger listened, shaking his head as though unable to comprehend the tragic accident. Again Chance sensed something about the man that he couldn't place a finger on. Balinger's reaction was the correct one, but it was slightly askew—as though it was the charade of a man who had observed the behavior of others in a similar situation and merely mimicked them.

When Defoe finally got around to mentioning the man at Elouise's window again, Chance added, "I think this man could very well be the ghostly visitor who intruded on Friday's dinner."

For an instant the gambler caught a spark of light within the depths of Balinger's jet eyes. A hint of a smug, amused smile hung at the corners of the man's mouth.

However, when he spoke, just the correct amount of surprise and befuddlement were in his voice. "And you say that you followed this Indian to my farm?"

"He should have exited the bayou shortly before Mr. Sharpe and me," Defoe answered with a confirming nod.

"Your Indian must have eluded you in the bayou, gentlemen," Balinger said with a shrug and a purse of his lips. "I've been sitting outside on the porch for the past hour or so, enjoying this unusual warmth. I assure you that I would have taken note of anyone coming onto my property—especially a half-naked savage wearing nothing but a loincloth."

Defoe bit at his lower lip, drew a deep breath, and finally said, "My worst fears have been realized. I tried to convince Mr. Sharpe that we had lost the Indian's trail, but he insisted on following the path until its end. We've disturbed you long enough, Mr. Balinger, and must return to the duties at hand."

Chance once more saw the glint in Balinger's eyes and the hint of a smile that reminded him of oil spreading atop water as the detective slightly dipped his head toward the man, then turned and started from the room.

The gambler reached out and shook Balinger's hand; it was oddly cold for such a humid day. "I appreciate your time and the bourbon."

"And I enjoyed the visit. Please come back when you have more time. I would be delighted to let you examine my collection at your leisure," the man said while he escorted them back to the porch. As the two men moved down the stairs and started toward the bayou, he called, "Please tell Elouise and Anne to call on me if there's anything they need during their time of sorrow."

Chance glanced back and waved at the man, unable to shake the sensation that Balinger was hiding something or someone. The gambler caught Defoe's expression out of the corner of an eye. From the deep furrows that creased the small man's brow, he was willing to bet that similar thoughts were plaguing the detective.

"Will you be returning to New Orleans today, Mr. Sharpe?" Defoe abruptly asked after they had covered half the distance back to the Walsh plantation.

Chance noted the return of the "Mr." before his name. "A taxi will be picking me up this afternoon."

"I'd like to catch a ride with you, if you don't mind? It would give me the opportunity to look around the Walsh estate a bit more without delaying the departure of the five officers who arrived with me."

Chance smiled. "If you don't mind being seen with a man you believe murdered three people, you're welcome to share my cab."

"If I can stop another member of the Walsh family from being killed," the detective answered, "I'd ride with the Devil himself."

FIFTEEN

Chance stared out the windows of the cab as Homer urged Bad Bad through the New Orleans evening. The day's soaking humidity had transformed to the night's fog as the air cooled. The glow of street lamps in the heavy mist reminded the gambler of a passage from Dickens where the English author had described London cloaked in fog. Not that Chance could verify the writer's authenticity; his only excursion beyond the borders of the United States had been his youthful sea voyage to the California gold fields.

"Whoa, Bad Bad," Homer called out from above as he drew the dappled gray mare to a halt outside Philip Duwayne's home.

Chance pushed from the hack's leather seat and stepped to the paved street. "Wait for me, Homer. I'll want to return to the Walsh estate after I've talked with Mr. Duwayne."

Homer grinned down at the gambler from beneath a brown bowler with a daffodil stuck beneath its band. "Me and Bad Bad ain't goin' nowheres till you give us the word."

The gambler smiled as he turned and walked toward the attorney's home. One of these days he would have to ask the cabbie the source of his never-ending supply of flowers—especially in the dead of winter!

Clarice answered the door and led Chance into her employer's study, where Philip sat with his feet propped on a hassock while he read a legal brief. The moment he saw the gambler, he started to rise.

"Don't get up," Chance halted his friend. "What I need you to look over can be done from that chair." He reached into a coat pocket and extracted two pieces of folded paper and handed them to the young lawyer. "Tell me if there's anyone questionable there."

"What is this?" Philip opened the sheets and began to scan them.

"A list of the guests at the Walsh plantation last weekend," Chance replied. "Anne Walsh drew it up for me."

"I've been reading in the *Picayune* about the Walsh deaths. A mother and her son in the space of three days; it's quite a tragedy. There's even rumors about malevolent spirits surrounding their deaths," Philip said. "The whole city is intrigued."

"Three deaths," Chance said, describing Warren's accident. "But I'm not here about Warren. I want to know if there's someone on that list that shouldn't be."

Philip shook his head. "Every man and woman listed here gets my nod of approval. They're all members in good standing of New Orleans high society. And all terribly boring. Are you certain the Walshes aren't yawning themselves to death? The only man of interest on this list is Michael Balinger."

The gambler's eyebrows arched. "Balinger? Is there something about him that I should know?"

"If you mean, does he have a dark, sinister past, no." Philip nodded to his liquor cabinet and indicated that Chance should pour them a drink. While he did, the attorney said, "Captain Michael Balinger is a native of New Orleans—about your age, I'd guess. During the war, he was quite a roguish figure in this city."

"A rogue, you say?" Chance handed his friend a bourbon and took a sip from the one he poured himself.

"A certified and notarized rogue, if there ever was one. He refused to don the Confederate gray and kept a sea captain's hat on his head," Philip said. "He became a blockade runner—supplied everything from arms to tobacco to New Orleans at exorbitant prices. Others who did the same were labeled crooks and swindlers, not Balinger. The men envisioned him as some heroic figure defying the Yankees, and the women adored him."

"And," Chance pressed.

"And that's about it," Philip replied with a shrug. "That's it?"

"Except for a rather lackluster end to his seafaring career," Philip said. "About six months before the end of the war, Balinger lost his ship off the coast of Brazil. He returned to New Orleans two months after the war ended in the company of a South American Indian as a manservant, bought a small piece of land, and declared himself retired."

Chance's head cocked to one side. "I visited Balinger's farm today and I didn't see an Indian manservant."

"You wouldn't," Philip answered. "A few months after Balinger's return, the Indian caused a bit of a scandal when he got in trouble with the police."

"What kind of trouble?" Chance was willing to wager that Balinger's manservant was also the ghost who had cursed Graham Walsh and his family Friday night.

"I don't remember the details. Something involving a young Negro woman, I think."

Any suggestions where I might find out those details?"

Philip sipped at the bourbon and shook his head. "Other than the police, I can't think of anyplace. It wasn't important enough to make the papers."

A dispute involving an Indian and a black woman wouldn't have been, not in New Orleans, Chance thought as he accepted the list Philip handed back to him. Under normal circumstances he would ask Philip to see what he could dig out of the police, but with Defoe having all but arrested, tried, and hanged him for murdering three members of the Walsh family, the gambler decided to try other avenues to find out what he could about Balinger's former manservant.

"Philip, you've helped more than you know," Chance said. "Now I'll take it from here. Have a good night."

"You're leaving?" The attorney sat up as the gambler started for the door to the study. "Where are you going?"

Chance stopped at the doorway, turned, and shrugged. "I'm not certain, but I'll know when I get there."

Chance had Homer wander aimlessly along New Orleans's avenues while he sat within the taxi, attempting to determine his next step. An hour pondering the facts that Philip had provided did not offer an easy avenue to uncovering the background on Balinger's Indian manservant.

"Mr. Chance, you made up your mind where you'd like me to take you yet?" Homer asked from atop the hack.

"To an Indian who got himself into trouble with a black girl," Chance answered glumly.

"What'd'ya say, Mr. Chance?" Homer's voice rose an octave.

"I said that I'm looking for an Indian from South America who got himself into trouble with the police over a Negro woman shortly after the war was over," Chance answered.

"Whoa, Bad Bad!" Homer tugged on the reins, drawing his mare to an abrupt halt. He leaned down, staring at the gambler. "You talkin' about the Mojo Man, Mr. Chance?"

"The Mojo Man?" The gambler looked up into the face of the cabbie hanging upside down outside the window. "What are you talking about, Homer?"

"The Mojo Man's the only Indian I knowed that got himself messed up with a black woman," the cabbie answered. "Only he ain't no real Indian, but an Indian from them jungles down in South America. His real name's Kalitisca, but all that knows him calls him the Mojo Man 'cause of all the magicks he works."

Chance sat straight in the taxi's seat. "The Indian that I'm looking for used to be a manservant to a Captain Michael Balinger before he was fired because of this girl."

"Don't know the name of the man the Mojo Man worked for, but if he was a sea captain, then I bet Kalitisca is the Indian you're lookin' for," Homer said.

"You're certain this Kalitisca was in trouble with the police because of his involvement with a black girl?"

"The same one that stole Tye Watson's wife Callie. The Mojo Man's a mean 'un, Mr. Chance. Most folks say that he walks hand in hand with the Devil himself. And anyone in New Orleans that knows anything about spirits has heard of the Mojo Man." Homer explained that Kalitisca caught the eye of a young woman married to a Negro by the name of Tye Watson. "Some say that the Mojo Man cast a spell on Callie to win her away from Tye and make her move in and live with him. I don't know about that, but I've knowed

Tye Watson most of my life. Tye don't take kindly to no man foolin' 'round with what is his.''

Homer then described the trouble Kalitisca had gotten into—Tye had come after him with a knife. "He was going to cut the Mojo Man's heart out and make him eat 'fore he died. Tye would have done what he set out to do, if'n some policeman hadn't been passing by and heard the Mojo Man call for help.''

Tye Watson was arrested, tried, convicted, and sentenced to two years in prison, Homer concluded his story. "Another six months and Tye will be out. 'Spect he'll finish what he started when he gets back in town.''

"What about Watson's wife, Callie?'' Chance asked, realizing Tye would be no help in locating Balinger's former servant. "I'd like to talk with her too, if it's possible.''

"That's the strange thing,'' Homer said, doing his best to shrug while hanging half upside down. "After the man shipped Tye off to the pen, Callie just up and disappeared all of a sudden like. The police investigated, but they couldn't find out nothing. Rumor is the Mojo Man kilt her. Some say that he even et her body like one of them cannibals. Ain't nobody can prove either. All anyone knows is Callie ain't 'round no more.''

"And this Kalitisca, is he still in New Orleans?'' Chance asked.

"Last time I heard, he was. Has a shack out on the edge of town,'' Homer replied. "It ain't like it was the gospel I'm tellin' you. Me, I stay clear of the Mojo Man. Don't even want to be in the same part of the city he's in. Not that I believe in all that haint and spirit talk, you understand? However, the way I see it, there ain't no call to go lookin' for trouble if'n you can avoid it.''

"I want you to drive me to Kalitisca's home, Homer," Chance said.

"When?" The cabbie's eyes grew white and round.

"Right now. As soon as you can get there," the gambler replied, waving the man forward.

"I'll do it, Mr. Chance, but just you remember that it was me who warned you away, if the Mojo Man lays a curse on your head." Homer's face disappeared from the window, and he called out, "Gitup, Bad Bad."

As the taxi jostled forward, Chance sank back in the cushions. He didn't have time to worry about Homer's imagined black magicks and curses. Right now he was out to break the curse that was quickly destroying the Walsh family!

Kalitisca's shack was just that, a shack. Constructed from old boards, the ten-by-ten single-room structure looked as though it would collapse with the first good blow off the Gulf of Mexico.

Chance found a half-burned candle in a holder made from a tin can atop an empty crate that served as a makeshift table set at the center of the shack. Striking a match, he lit the candle and held it over his head.

The flickering yellow light did nothing to improve the shack's condition. Besides a dilapidated cot with a frayed, straw-stuffed mattress, two chairs made from wooden crates and a matching table, there was no furniture in the room. However, several shaky-appearing shelves had been nailed to the wall. Each of these was stacked with various jars and vials. The gambler opened a dozen or more of the containers and quickly stuffed their corks back into their necks. Each container contained foul-smelling substances that the Indian used in his various supernatural rites, Chance decided.

The only other thing he noticed was the dust; it lay at least an inch thick over everything in the shack—including the floor. If Kalitisca lived here, it had been weeks since he last visited his home.

Brushing his palms together to remove the dust on them, Chance walked outside where Homer waited. The cabbie stood beside his hack, talking to a black man who leaned on a crooked cane.

"This here's Wilmer Dallas," Homer introduced the man when Chance joined them. "He lives on down the road a piece. Wilmer was on his way home when he noticed Bad Bad and me and the light you lit in the shack. Wilmer stopped to see what was up. He told me that the Mojo Man ain't been home for over a month now and ain't nobody knows where he's gone."

"Or cares," Wilmer added with decided conviction. "A good man ain't got no call to go askin' after a bad one."

Chance normally would have agreed, but in this case he was certain Kalitisca was the key to the three members of the Walsh family who had died.

"Mr. Chance." Homer nudged the gambler and pointed back toward New Orleans. "It looks like we got official-type company."

A police paddy wagon rolled down the dirt road and halted beside the taxi. Detective Jean Defoe stared down at the gambler from the driver's box. "Mr. Sharpe; may I ask what you are doing here?"

Chance quickly explained the events that had led him to the shack. Defoe drew a heavy breath and slowly exhaled it, then admitted that after their meeting with Balinger, he had recalled the incident involving the former sea captain's manservant.

"We both arrived too late," Chance said as he climbed into the taxi. "Kalitisca hasn't been here in over a month—ask Mr. Dallas there."

"A month, maybe longer, that he's been gone," the man said before the officer could ask.

"Mr. Sharpe," Defoe called out as the gambler ordered Homer to drive back to the Walsh plantation, "you're treading on dangerous ground. This is police business. I warn you not to interfere in an official investigation. Leave Kalitisca and Balinger to me, or you might find yourself facing charges of obstructing justice."

"I thought that you'd ruled the Walsh deaths accidental," Chance shouted from the cab's window as it trundled away. "I didn't realize there was an official investigation under way!"

SIXTEEN

Anne Walsh was the only member of her rapidly diminishing family awake when Homer halted his dappled gray mare outside the mansion. She rushed from the house and threw her arms around the gambler as he stepped from the taxi, clutching him in her trembling arms.

Chance held her close for several minutes, stroking her hair and whispering that everything would be all right—and hoping she believed words he had no faith in—before he released her and asked the cabbie if he would spend the night. When Homer agreed, Anne ordered one of the servants to take the man to the stables where he could bed down Bad Bad and then to guest quarters behind the mansion. As the taxi rolled away, Chance walked into the main house with Anne still clinging to him.

"It's late," he said when they reached the stair leading to the mansion's upper story. "You should have been in bed hours ago."

Anne shook her head. "I tried to sleep, but I couldn't without you. Mother, James, and Warren wouldn't leave my mind. I just can't accept that they're gone. Everything has turned upside down. All that was beautiful is suddenly dark and terrifying, Chance. Things like this just don't happen—not without a reason."

With his arm about her shoulders, he led her up the curving stairway to his bedroom and closed the door behind them. He agreed with her. The Walsh family butchery was not without reason; however, he had yet to discover that reason, nor was he certain that he could before death claimed everyone in the house. His only hope had been the Indian Kalitisca, but unless he figured the situation wrong, Kalitisca was hiding somewhere in the bayou, waiting for Balinger to give him his next order.

If Balinger is the man behind these murders, he thought. The fact that the police had not discovered any evidence did nothing to bolster his theory that the three Walshes had been murdered.

"Chance, is there a curse?" Anne asked while she disrobed and pulled back the bed covers. "Is Father right? Has this family been cursed?"

He watched her slip into the bed and tug the covers beneath her chin to hide her nakedness. "There's no curse, Anne. What's happening to your family is *real* and has nothing to do with the supernatural. I've talked with Detective Defoe, and he believes the same thing. He's investigating the case at this very moment." He carefully avoided mentioning that he was the detective's prime suspect.

Anne's gaze hung on the ceiling while he pulled off his clothes and tossed them across a chair. "Defoe seems like a good-hearted man, but is he capable of discovering who's behind the murders? After all, he has already ruled the deaths were either accidental—or from natural causes, as in Mother's case."

"I told you that he believes they were all murders now and is handling the case accordingly." The gambler slid into the bed and gathered her into his arms.

Her lips found his, but there was no passion in her embrace, nor did he force his own desire on her. Instead, he held her close until her eyes fluttered closed and her breathing shallowed to the gentle rhythm of sleep.

Sleep did not come so easy for him. He lay on his back with Anne nestled on his shoulder, staring at the patterns the moonlight, night breeze, and trees made on the ceiling. His mind refused to let loose of Captain Michael Balinger. The man had been hiding something earlier today, he was certain of that; had read it in his smug little smile. But what? And where?

Chance awoke from a listless sleep with the first rays of dawn that filtered through the bedroom's windows. Balinger remained on his mind. There was no sense in delaying the inevitable; he had to meet with the former sea captain again—although he wasn't certain what to say or how to say it. If necessary, he realized, he would openly confront the man with the murders, claiming he could prove that he had committed them.

Then sit back and see what develops, he thought. Defoe wouldn't approve of his tactics, but then he wasn't a "trained and experienced sleuth" as was Jean Defoe.

Easing his left arm from beneath Anne's head, the gambler inched to the edge of the bed and swung his legs over the side. He stood, bringing a soft moan from the young woman's lips. However, her eyes didn't open, and she slipped back into sleep. On tiptoes he crossed the room and dressed as quietly as possible, leaving his boots off until he walked into the hall.

In the kitchen the cook was busily preparing breakfast for the house's staff. Grabbing two links of spicy sausage from a platter she filled, he stuffed them between two biscuits. Jam or honey would have been nice on the sandwiches, but there was no time. He wanted to confront Balinger as soon as possible, wanted to catch the man off guard before he was fully awake.

Exiting the mansion through the rear door, he hastened toward the bayou and the path that led to Balinger's small farm.

Chance tugged the bell attached to the front door of Balinger's home—three times. When no answer came from within, he rapped his right knuckles against the door's wood, firmly. Still there was no answer.

With lips pursed in doubt, the gambler walked to the end of the long front porch and stepped to the winter-yellowed lawn. He walked behind the house to a small barn whose single sliding door lay drawn back. Neither horse nor man was inside.

"Damn!" A frustrated curse pushed past Chance's lips. He was certain that he had risen early enough to catch the former schooner captain at home.

The gambler's steely blue eyes surveyed the fields surrounding house and barn, hoping to glimpse the farm's owner. All he saw were close-cropped pastures of grass.

Chance's eyes narrowed. A half-forgotten memory pushed from the back of his mind. The night Anne had introduced him to Balinger, the man had mentioned trying to develop a new strain of rice. This parcel of land might have once held grazing animals such as horses and cattle, but it had never produced a single stalk of rice. Paddies aflood with water were required to grow rice!

Why would Balinger lie about his farm? Chance shook his head; he had no answers. Nor could he even call these open fields a farm. They were merely pasture that gave no indication that they had been touched by a plow or a harrow in recent years. *If he isn't farming, what is he doing here?*

The answer to that question wedged solidly into the gambler's mind. Balinger never had any intention of using the land. This farm gave him the one thing that he needed to carry out his real purpose—close proximity to the Walsh plantation!

Walking back to the house's front door, Chance pounded on the wood and called out to its owner. When no one answered, he tried the latch. The door swung inward. The gambler entered without hesitation.

Balinger's home was tidy and neat—perhaps too much so for a man living alone. Had he not known who resided within, Chance would have attributed the immaculate parlor, bedrooms, kitchen, den, and study to an old maid rather than to a man who once had sailed the high seas. It was as though the house had just been put in readiness for a future owner, but now was vacant.

Careful to replace every item back in its exact resting spot, Chance searched the entire home, beginning with the parlor. He worked his way through the house, ending up in the only room that hinted a man dwelled within—Balinger's study, with its extensive collection of weapons on the wall.

Chance studied the four walls, and the implements of death that filled them. The longer he looked, the more ridiculous was Balinger's claim that the firearms and various blades were mere decorations. A man simply did not surround himself with rifles, swords, and knives unless he held a deep-seated love for such items. *And can use them.*

Stepping to a wall displaying an assortment of various sheathed blades, the gambler lifted a rapier from its wooden rack. He grasped the bejeweled hilt and slid the sword halfway from its scabbard. *Toledo steel,* he realized. There was no mistaking the superb craftsmanship that had produced the Spanish blade. Only the smiths of those distant and mysterious islands of Japan were known to produce swords of equal quality.

Replacing the rapier, Chance let his gaze rove over the wall. The variety of blades seemed endless. There were cutlasses with massive bell guards almost encompassing their hilts, slender fencing foils, a bastard sword with a one-and-a-half hand grip that was meant to be swung from the back of a mount, a curving-bladed scimitar with tiny rubies studding its pommel, a rusted ancient short sword that might have once been wielded by one of Julius Caesar's soldiers, and an assortment of strangely twisted swords for which Chance had no names.

Likewise, the small blades that hung beside their larger cousins ran the gamut from small palm knives that remained popular among the gamblers on the Mississippi to double-bladed knives with serrated edges.

As eye-catching as the swords and knives were the sheaths that held the various blades. Some were adorned with precious and semiprecious stones. Others flashed with silver and gold. Delicate engravings and intricate filigree work decorated another portion of the collection.

So impressive was Balinger's armory that a small, insignificant knife in a plain, brown leather scabbard almost escaped the gambler's attention—almost. Perhaps because the homely-appearing knife seemed out of place among the obviously expensive weapons, it drew Chance's eye.

Lifting the knife from the peg that held it, he wrapped his fingers around its wooden handle and pulled it from its sheath. The gambler's heart pounded. The blade was carved from wood!

"Son of a bitch!" The curse whistled between his clenched teeth.

The curved blade might have been a brother to the one that St. Louis Detective Colbert Marshal had given him as his souvenir of the alley attack that had almost cost him his life. *Or a sister to the one used against Warren Walsh on the* Wild Card*!*

If the gambler had held any doubts that Balinger was behind the death of Rachael Walsh and her two sons, they evaporated as he shoved the wooden knife back into its scabbard. For a moment, he considered taking the blade with him, then decided against it. The authorities had to find the knife exactly where Balinger had hung it.

Chance carefully slipped the knife back on its peg. This wasn't what he had come for, but it was enough. He had to get back to the Walsh plantation and awake Homer to drive him to New Orleans where he would talk with Jean Defoe.

SEVENTEEN

Detective Jean Defoe, dressed in a black suit with a red rosebud on his lapel, stood at the kitchen door. The police officer's right arm rose and signaled Chance forward when the gambler emerged from the bayou.

"I thought that you had been properly warned to keep away from official police business last night." Defoe began his reprimand before Chance reached the steps that led to the door. "You realize that the offense of obstructing justice can carry a prison term in this state, don't you?"

"I was just out for my morning constitutional, Defoe," Chance replied. "I don't believe that a stroll is against the law in Louisiana—at least, not yet."

"I think that a judge would find a visit with Captain Michael Balinger questionable," the detective said. "Especially in light of the developing situation."

"Who said that I was visiting with Balinger?" Chance edged past the investigator into the kitchen, found a cup, and poured himself a coffee.

"You weren't talking with Captain Balinger?" Defoe stared at the gambler in disbelief. "Why else would you be in the bayou?"

Chance rolled his eyes and casually perused the ceiling. "I might have been studying the flora and fauna."

"But you weren't."

"No," the gambler finally admitted. "I went to confront Balinger with the murders to see if I could stir him up enough to make a mistake. Trouble was, the captain wasn't at home."

"Thank God!" The detective gusted a sign of relief. "You would have ruined everything."

"So I took a look around his house instead," Chance added.

"What?" Defoe's eyes grew round, then narrowed. "That's breaking and entering!"

"Not if the front door is unlocked," Chance replied between leisurely sips of the steaming coffee. "Besides, I found something that links Balinger to the attempts on Anne's and Warren's lives—a wooden knife exactly like the one used by their assailants."

"Are you certain?"

"It's hanging right on a wall in his study along with the rest of that small arsenal he never uses," Chance explained. "I left the blade on the wall so that you could see where he has it. Don't want to interfere with an official investigation, you know."

"Interesting, very interesting." A smug little smile set the ends of the detective's upturned mustache to quivering. "Almost as interesting as certain information that I've uncovered, concerning our Captain Balinger."

It was Chance's turn for his eyes to narrow in interest. "What information?"

Defoe milked the moment for all it was worth. While the gambler waited, he requested a cup of tea—with cream and sugar—from the Walshes' cook. He waited until the woman had put a kettle on to boil before turning back to Chance and saying:

"After I saw you last night outside Kalitisca's shack, I had a late dinner with an old friend of mine, a professor at Tulane whose hobby is the various Indian cultures of South America. Before the war he had made several expeditions into the Amazon jungle.''

''And?'' Chance attempted to hasten the detective toward his point.

''And he informed me that the use of a certain poison—curare, to be exact, is common among many of the jungle tribes. They dip the tips of their arrows and darts, which they blow through hollow tubes, in this curare. The poison somehow affects the nerves that are related to the muscles, causing the muscles to relax. Strangely enough, curare may be either eaten or drunk without it harming an individual, but even a small amount introduced into the bloodstream can be deadly,'' Defoe explained. ''A victim of this poison finds that every muscle in his body just relaxes and he loses control.''

''Including the heart.'' Chance followed the detective's train of thought to its obvious conclusion.

''Precisely,'' Defoe said with a nod. ''If you recall, Balinger's schooner wrecked off the coast of Brazil. He would have had ample opportunity to become acquainted with curare and its lethal effects.''

''Kalitisca would have supplied him with the poison,'' Chance added.

''My thoughts exactly.'' Defoe smiled at the gambler, then accepted his tea from the cook. He took a long sip before he said, ''There's more.''

''More?''

The detective took another sip from the cup. ''While you were on your morning constitutional, I was at the parish courthouse. Since a large portion of records were destroyed during the war, I really didn't expect to find anything. However . . .''

Defoe reached into his coat and extracted a piece of paper that he passed to the gambler. Chance arched a questioning eyebrow as he unfolded the document. His expression transformed to one of confusion as he scanned the paper.

"It's Balinger's birth certificate. What bearing does this have on anything?" Chance glanced at the detective, then read over the birth certificate again. The second reading located what the first missed. "It's marked 'bastard'!"

"The surprise in your voice echoes my own reaction," Defoe said with that smug smile returning to his thin lips. "However, my surprise tripled when I questioned a clerk about the authenticity of that document. He assured me that Michael Balinger was indeed born a bastard, and that the circumstances surrounding his birth had been considered quite a scandal in New Orleans society thirty-five years ago."

While Chance listened, Defoe recounted all that the clerk had said. Balinger's mother had been a belle in her day, with beaus and suitors coming to call from ten parishes away. The young beauty, a mere tender fifteen years of age, seemed to show no interest in all the men who wooed her.

"Then one morning her mother noticed that her lovely daughter was in a family way," the detective said. "Try as her parents did, the girl refused to divulge the name of the scoundrel who had so indelibly left his mark on her until-then-spotless young life. Nor would the girl agree to marry any one of twenty men who were only too willing to make her an honest woman. Stubbornly she delivered her son out of wedlock and died in the process. Michael Balinger was raised by his grandparents, much to their embarrassment and shame."

"I seem to be missing something, Defoe," Chance said. "I still don't see what Balinger's questionable heritage has to do with the Walsh murders."

"What if I told you that Graham Walsh was considered to be the favorite candidate for the girl's less-than-honorable lover?"

"Graham Walsh?" Chance couldn't believe what he heard. "Are you certain?"

"That was the rumor. No other names were ever mentioned, according to the clerk," Defoe replied. "If Walsh is indeed Balinger's father, a motive for his crimes becomes quite clear."

More than clear, Chance thought. Men had killed others for wealth throughout the ages. Balinger was simply following in their footsteps.

"I believe that we should have a discussion with Mr. Graham Walsh about a certain illegitimate son, don't you, Mr. Sharpe?" The detective glanced upward toward the mansion's second story.

"Exactly what I was thinking," Chance said as he walked from the kitchen, down the hall, and up the stairs.

It was Defoe who knocked on the elder Walsh's bedroom door. His answer was a noncommittal grunt of recognition from the man inside. "Mr. Walsh, this is Detective Defoe. I apologize for disturbing you, but I must have a word with you."

"Go away," Graham answered in a voice that sounded distant. Chance could imagine the man huddled in his chair with the Colt in hand.

"Please, Mr. Walsh, I must insist that you allow me in," Defoe persisted. "It has to do with your family."

"Go away!" Fear tinged Graham's tone. "You can't come in, and I'm sure as hell not coming out."

"Mr. Walsh . . ." Defoe began again.

"Unless you want me to open up with this scatter-gun, I suggest that you get away from my door," Graham shouted. "No one, and I mean no one, is coming close to me!"

"Defoe—" Chance took the detective's shoulder and edged him away from the bedroom's locked door. "It's no good. He'll never let us in. Even if he did, I doubt that he'd talk sense. Listen to his voice; he's gone over the edge."

The policeman glanced at the door and then at Chance before tilting his head in agreement. "You're right. We'll get nothing out of him."

Chance pursed his lips, then smiled. "Balinger won't know that—not if we tell him that Graham revealed that the captain was his illegitimate son."

A grin slowly spread across the short detective's face. "Devious, Mr. Sharpe, very devious, but it just might work."

Michael Balinger opened the door to his home when Chance knocked on the front door. A touch of amusement sparked in the man's eyes when he saw the gambler and the policeman. "Gentlemen, this visit is quite a surprise. I didn't think you'd accept my invitation to view my weapons collection so soon."

"Your collection is just one of the things I'm interested in, Balinger." Defoe pushed past Chance and entered the house. "But the weapons are as good a place to begin as any. Shall we adjourn to your study?"

"Certainly." Balinger waved an arm toward the house's interior. "I believe you know the way."

The amusement in Balinger's dark eyes seemed to glow now. If he had an idea of why the detective visited him, it apparently had no effect on the man, Chance noted.

Inside the study Defoe walked to the wall covered with swords and knives. After a few moments, he lifted the wooden-bladed knife from its peg, pulled it from the leather sheath, and held it up so that Balinger could see the weapon. "An interesting blade."

"One similar to those used in the attacks on Anne and Warren Walsh during their recent trip, I believe," Balinger said. "The knife is used by certain Indian tribes in the South American jungles. Although those savages usually dip the blade in a poison called curare. Nasty stuff that, odorless, tasteless, but extremely deadly."

"Then you know of the attacks on Anne and Warren?" Defoe pounced on the man's revelation.

"Of course I do," Balinger replied with a touch of enjoyment in his tone as he settled into a chair behind the room's desk. "I *am* the Walshes' neighbor. There isn't much that happens to that family of which I am not aware."

"Is that because you happen to be a member of the Walsh family yourself?" Defoe surprised Chance by taking the direct route to the matter that had brought them here.

Balinger chuckled and leaned back into the chair. "How did you find out that Graham Walsh was my father, Detective? I thought only he and I knew for certain. And, of course, my mother, but then she's been dead for as long as I can remember."

Equally surprising to the gambler was Balinger's open admission that he was Graham Walsh's bastard son. If the man had killed Rachael and her two sons, he seemed to be unconcerned with Defoe's having uncovered his link to the family.

Abruptly Balinger began to laugh. The sound and the motions seemed to be right, but something was missing from his sudden merriment, Chance sensed. It was as though there was no feeling behind the laughter—only the sound and the gesture.

"Ah, I see! I see!" Balinger continued to laugh. "First the knife and now the fact that Graham Walsh sired a son out of wedlock. The pieces begin to fall into place, Detective Defoe. You think that *I* am responsible for Rachael's, James's and Warren's deaths—that I murdered them!''

Again the man laughed, pointing a finger at the policeman. ''This is rich, my friend. And what are my motives? Wait, don't tell me. Let me guess? The revenge of a shunned son? No, far too trite. Hate for what Graham Walsh did to my mother? No, that's not it either, since I never knew my mother. What could it be?''

Balinger grinned at Defoe, who shifted his weight from one foot to the other as though in discomfort. ''It has to be something appropriate for a mental giant such as you to conceive of, Detective. Yes, that's it. It's certainly mundane and unimaginative enough to suit your small mind. I am killing off the members of the Walsh family one by one so that I will eventually inherit Graham Walsh's fortune by virtue of being his only living relative.''

''Do you deny it?'' The policeman refused to be shaken by Balinger's outrageous performance.

''Deny it? Why should I, Detective Defoe?'' Balinger's grin widened.

To Chance it was obvious that the man was playing cat and mouse with the policeman and enjoying every minute of it. It was also obvious that he realized that they knew he was the killer and simply didn't care.

''You have done all the denying for me that needs to be done, Defoe,'' the man continued. ''In each of the three deaths, you have ruled that the Walshes died of natural causes or that their lives were cut short by accidents.''

''My investigation is an ongoing one, Balinger,'' Defoe replied. ''The book hasn't been closed yet.''

Balinger laughed once again. This time Chance detected contempt in the man's tone and in the blaze of his dark eyes.

"What do you want from me, Detective? Do you wish for me to confess that I somehow arranged for the ghostly visitor who intruded the Walsh dinner party last weekend?"

"The apparition was your former manservant, Balinger, an Indian from Brazil named Kalitisca," Chance interjected. "He was the man Defoe and I chased to your house yesterday morning."

Balinger ignored the gambler, his gaze locked to the policeman. "Or do you want me to breakdown and admit how I rode beside James the day of the hunt? How, when he asked me to hold his shotgun for him while he lit a cigar, I turned the gun on him and blew his head from his shoulder?"

The man paused when Defoe opened his mouth. When the detective could do no more than mutter several incoherent mumblings, Balinger started in again. "No I think you want me to confess that I used a South American poison—the same the Indians use on their wooden knives—on the bristles of Rachael Walsh's hairbrush, so that when she brushed her graying hair, her scalp was ever so gently nipped to allow the poison to enter her bloodstream and still her heart."

"Curare works that way, Balinger. I should know; your men almost killed me with it in Saint Louis," Chance spoke up again when he realized that the man was outlining how he murdered the members of the Walsh family.

"And you, Sharpe"—Balinger's gaze shifted to the gambler as though he no longer found a challenge in the stammering detective—"I bet you would be delighted if I were to detail how I located that lightning-struck tree and its fallen branch the morning of the hunt; how I used my former manservant to lure Warren into the bayou where I waited to impale his heart. Yes, I believe that both of you would enjoy that, but . . .''

Balinger paused, apparently relishing the melodramatic moment that mounted, ''. . . none of that is to be, gentlemen. All you will get from me is contempt! If you want proof of foul play, then find it yourselves. And until you do, don't return to this house. Do I make myself clear? Neither of you is welcome here, so please leave—immediately.''

''You've made yourself totally clear,'' Chance said. ''But let me make myself clear—you killed three members of the Walsh family, and for that I intend to see you hang if it's the last thing I do.''

''And you, Sharpe, are a bigger fool than this sawed-off little man who claims to be a police detective,'' Balinger said with a laugh. ''Now get out of my house!''

Neither Chance nor Defoe said another word as they turned and left Balinger's home. Both glanced over their shoulders when they reentered the bayou, as though vowing that they would return with the evidence needed to send the man to the gallows.

EIGHTEEN

"He taunted me!" Defoe's long-held silence broke with a vehement burst of disgust. "The blackheart sat there goading and taunting me!"

"Us," Chance corrected while his mind repeated the scene in Balinger's office time after time. The man had actually sat there and openly described how he had committed each of the murders—including coating the bristles of Rachael Walsh's hairbrush with the poison curare!

"The gall of the whoreson! Not only did he give me his motive and methods, but he threw them into my face like a glove that demands satisfaction." The detective continued to spew out his exasperation. Defoe abruptly stopped and turned to the gambler. "I am afraid that I made a terrible mistake in my earlier accusations, Mr. Sharpe. I allowed coincidence to blind me to the truth."

"Chance. Call me Chance," the gambler answered, then added: "Those coincidences were all neatly planned, unless I miss my bet about Balinger. He needed someone as a scapegoat, someone to divert attention from his own actions. I just happened by and was unlucky enough to be selected for the role."

"Insidious! The original attacks on Anne and Warren weren't supposed to succeed. They were merely a diversionary tactic to sidetrack my investigation while

Balinger carried out the Walsh curse," Defoe said, following Chance's line of thought.

"I just happened to be in the right place at the wrong time. Balinger took full advantage of it," Chance said with a shake of his head. It was as the detective had said—insidious.

Defoe began walking again, his eyes downcast as though studying the path. "Balinger is not a totally sane man; he believes himself above the law—untouchable."

"With good reason," Chance said. "His crimes have been perfect. He's left no evidence of his actions, and he damn well knows it."

"No crime is perfect." The small detective shook his head. "Balinger has made a mistake somewhere. My task is to uncover that mistake."

"Kalitisca?" Chance suggested.

"Perhaps." Defoe nodded. "If Balinger doesn't manage to eliminate the Indian before I can find him."

"Before *we* find him. I don't like another man using me while he goes around killing people. I'm in this whether you like it or not, Defoe." Chance watched the policeman draw a heavy breath, slowly exhale, and finally nod in acceptance. "At least we accomplished something this morning. Now that Balinger knows we're on to him, he won't try to harm the rest of the Walsh family."

"I am not as certain of that as you, Chance. I fear that he considers us merely a minor distraction and will attempt to fulfill the Walsh curse." The detective shook his head when the two men reached the end of the path. "Balinger is not like other men; you can see that in his eyes. Human feelings are alien to him. He dwells in a world that centers on Michael Balinger— nothing but his own wants and desires matter. The murders are a game to him in which he proves his superiority to those of us who admit that we are mere mortals."

"Detective Defoe!" A man, his voice strained with tension, hailed the policeman as the two started for the Walsh mansion. "Detective Defoe, please hurry. There's been another terrible accident."

Chance looked up to see the butler waving them forward. The gambler broke into a full run with Defoe matching his pace.

"Upstairs," the butler said when they reached the back door. "It's Mr. Walsh. He's collapsed in his bedroom the same way Mrs. Walsh did."

"Damn!" Chance moved into the house behind the detective, following him upstairs to Graham's bedroom.

The elder Walsh lay on the floor in front of a washstand. Steam still rose from the water in the basin, and a shaving cup stood thick with creamy lather. An open razor was inches from the dead man's fingers. Anne and Elouise were in a corner of the room clutching each other; their eyes brimmed with horror as they stared at their father's unmoving body. Outside, the servants gathered behind the butler and the maid Alita, necks craning to catch a glimpse of the fallen man.

"Shaving?" Defoe questioned as he rose from beside Graham's body. "What was he doing shaving? How did this hot water get into his room?"

"He called for it." Anne looked at the detective and then at Chance. "After you two left, Father opened the door to his room and summoned Elouise and me. He said that he had been acting like a crazy man, and that he was ready to return to the world. He then ordered Alita to bring him up a kettle of hot water. He said he was going to shave, then come down for breakfast."

"And you brought the water?" the detective asked the maid as he knelt beside Graham again and began to closely examine the body.

"Yes, sir," Alita answered. "When I got here with the kettle, Mr. Graham told me to lay out his razor and soap, then start straightenin' up the mess in his room. I was doing just that when he fell down."

"I can see no signs of violence." Defoe shook his head; his mouth twisted with disgust. "It appears that he was shaving when he died, just as Alita said. See, there's a drop of blood on his neck where he nicked himself shortly before he collapsed."

"Nicked himself?" The phrase was like an alarm in the gambler's head.

His gaze darted to the minor cut the detective pointed to on Graham's neck, then to the razor beside the dead man. Lifting the steel blade by its handle, he examined the edge in the light of an open window. A film the hue of pale honey coated the razor's edge.

"Curare! Defoe, the razor's been doctored with curare!" Chance held the blade out for the policeman to examine.

The rustle of starched skirts snapped Defoe's head around. Alita pushed her way through the servants blocking the door. "Stop that woman!"

There was no difficulty in the task. The butler and a younger man in livery grabbed the woman's shoulders, halting her in mid-stride. In the next instant, she fell apart. Alita's body shuddered violently and tears rolled down her cheeks. "It was the demon. It wasn't me; it was the demon!"

"Sit her on the bed," Defoe ordered, watching while the maid was placed on the edge of the bed. "Now the rest of you please leave us alone. I must question this woman."

The butler edged the other servants, Anne, and Elouise away from the bedroom as the detective directed. However, Chance didn't move. Defoe gave him one glance, bit his lower lip, and nodded in silent acquiescence before turning to Alita. "What demon killed Mr. Walsh?"

The maid wiped at her cheeks. The action was ineffectual; another flood gushed from her eyes when she shuddered and sobbed, "The one that's been hauntin' me and my baby for the past two weeks!"

Between Alita's ever-flowing tears and sobs, and Defoe's relentless questioning, the maid's story gradually emerged. Twenty-two years old and a former slave, Alita lived with a three-year-old daughter in a house near the bayou. Two weeks ago a "demon-man" visited her home in the middle of the night.

"He used me," she sobbed. "Said he'd kill me if I didn't give him what he wanted. And when he was through, he beat me. He's come to me every night since then." She opened the collar of her dress to reveal purple-black bruises on her brown skin to show where the "demon-man" had beaten her repeatedly.

Through the detective's grilling questions, she described her supernatural tormentor as a short man with stringy hair that hung to his shoulders. He wore a piece of "flapping" leather between his legs that barely covered his genitalia and buttocks. However, because of the night's darkness, she never saw the demon's face.

"But he looked like the ghost that cursed Mr. Graham last Friday at the dinner party," Alita offered. "And his voice, it was the same."

"Kalitisca!" The name came from Chance's lips like a foul curse.

"Precisely." The detective nodded, then turned back to Alita. "But why did you poison Mr. and Mrs. Walsh?"

"I done said it was the demon," the maid pleaded. "He forced me to do his bidding. He stole my little Nina. He said that he'd kill her dead unless I done exactly what he said. He told me he'd beat her to death just like he beat me with his fists. Then he gave me this."

From a pocket of the apron she wore, Alita produced a wooden vial with a reed stopper in its mouth. Defoe opened the small container, smelled its contents, and passed it to the gambler. The thick, honeylike substance inside left no doubt that the vial contained deadly curare.

"And you spread this on Rachael Walsh's hairbrush the morning she died," the detective stated more than asked while he patted at his slicked-down hair.

"Just like the demon told me." Alita wiped at her tears again. "Then this morning I put it on Mr. Graham's razor. I was supposed to do that before now, but Mr. Graham went and locked himself away for the past few days."

And when he opened the door, the curse was waiting for him, Chance thought. Only there was no curse, just Balinger and his Indian accomplice, Kalitisca.

"I had to do it, don't you see? If'n I didn't, he said he'd kill my girl. There weren't nothing else I could do," Alita pleaded as her eyes rolled up to the detective.

"You might have told one of us about this 'demon-man,'" the detective said when he walked to the bedroom's door and opened it. To the butler who still waited outside, he asked, "Is there a room where this woman can be kept until I decide what to do with her?"

The butler nodded, then at Defoe's request led Alita away.

Chance watched the maid leave. *Insidious,* the word kept repeating in his mind.

NINETEEN

"Ladies." Detective Defoe turned to Anne and Elouise. "If we could step outside, I have something to explain to you."

The two sisters walked from the bedroom. The policeman drew a deep breath as though bolstering himself, then waved Chance after them. Outside, Defoe closed the door, took another steadying breath, and revealed all that he had learned and suspected about Balinger.

"No!" Elouise glared at the detective. "I won't believe that Father had a bastard son. I won't! He would never do something like that to us. Never, do you hear me? Never!"

With that, the woman swirled around and ran down the hall. She disappeared into her bedroom, slamming the door behind her.

Anne stared after her sister for a moment, then turned back to the two men. "I hope you both understand that Elouise isn't usually like this. Father's murder has driven her near the brink. If you'll go downstairs, I'll join you in a bit. I need to be alone with my sister now."

Chance and Defoe did as Anne requested, walking back to the kitchen for fresh cups of coffee and tea. As they took their respective drinks into the parlor and settled into chairs, the gambler asked, "What do you intend to do with Alita?"

"What I don't intend to do is press charges, unless one of those two sisters demands it," the detective said. "I'm hoping Alita will lead us to Kalitisca. Once I have the Indian, Balinger is mine."

"If Balinger doesn't get to Kalitisca first," Chance reminded the detective of his earlier comment.

"Those sisters upstairs are my hope that he won't." Defoe took a sip from his cup and paused for a moment as though gathering his thoughts. "Balinger has relied heavily on Kalitisca to do a large portion of his dirty work for him up to this point. If I were a wagering man such as you, Chance, I'd give odds that he won't eliminate the Indian until he has absolutely no further use of him. And as long as those two sisters are alive, Balinger has a use for Kalitisca."

Defoe might be right, Chance realized. But at the moment, he was more worried about Anne and Elouise than Kalitisca. The two women were the sole survivors of the Walsh family. Balinger would not hesitate to arrange their murders whenever it was convenient to him.

"Isn't there something you can do to lock Balinger away for a while?" Chance asked, feeling a sense of desperation closing in around him.

"I could have him brought in for questioning," the detective answered. "Under normal circumstances, I might be able to lose him in a cell for as long as a month. But a man like Balinger has prepared himself for such a maneuver. The moment I walked him into the station house, a well-paid lawyer would appear with all the necessary papers—signed by a judge whose palm had been lubricated with a generous under-the-table bribe—and walk Balinger right outside within a few hours."

The man was right, Chance realized, but it didn't help. Defoe should try something—*anything!* If he didn't, either Anne or Elouise—or both—would soon join the other members of their family in death.

"No! Elouise, you can't!" Anne's voice, filled with panic, echoed down the hall and into the parlor. "Elouise, please! Elouise!"

Coffee and tea forgotten, Chance and Defoe leaped to their feet and ran from the room. They found Anne collapsed at the top of the stairs, pointing to the open door of the mansion.

"It's Elouise! She's gone mad!" Anne shouted down to the men. "She's beyond reason. She kept repeating that it wasn't Balinger who killed Father, but the curse. She said that she had to get away before the curse killed her. Please stop her, Chance. She doesn't know what she's doing!"

The gambler pivoted and bolted out the door. Elouise was nowhere in sight. For a moment he stumbled, uncertain where to turn. But there was only one course to take, he recognized. A woman trying to escape the estate would need a mount.

Running around the house, his long strides carried him toward the low-slung stable a quarter of a mile away. Although he didn't see Elouise, he did see two grooms hastening toward an open stall. Before they could reach the wide door, a sleek black mare leaped for freedom with her head and tail held high as she ran.

Chance heard the groan from inside the stall an instant after the groom reached the door. Three strides later, he found its source. One of the grooms stumbled from the stall, clutching his gut. He barely made it past the gambler before he doubled over and emptied his stomach.

"She didn't have no business goin' in there alone." The second groom, his face as white as a sheet, staggered from the stall, shaking his head. "She knowed better than to go in there. That mare's a crazy one; ain't hardly broke."

Chance moved to the stall's door. His own stomach churned violently. Inside, Elouise's broken body lay crumpled atop the rice straw covering the stall's floor. Blood oozed from a score of wounds over her face and body.

"She knowed better." The groom behind the gambler stared back at the stall, when Chance turned from the scene. "She had horse sense like James. She knowed what a mare like that could do to her. Why'd she go in there like that? Tell me why she done it."

Chance merely shook his head. He had no explanation for the insanity—the fear—that had driven Elouise Walsh into the stall of a wild mare to die beneath the animal's hooves.

TWENTY

Anne's gold-flecked eyes lifted to study Chance's face. Doubt darkened her expression. "Are you sure this is the way it has to be? Won't you come with me?"

The gambler shook his head. "I have to stay here. Until Balinger is behind bars, I won't be able to breathe easy. But you'll be all right. An old friend of mine, Jason Haver, will meet you in Saint Louis. He'll see that you have a safe place to stay until this is over."

Anne nodded, then rose on her tiptoes to kiss the gambler's lips before she crossed the gangplank onto the *Wild Card*'s main deck. There Henri Tuojacque escorted her up to the boiler deck and into a stateroom.

"We'll see that she stays out of harm's way," Captain Bert Rooker called out as the riverboat's lines were cast away and the massive sidewheeler pulled out into the Mississippi's current. "Don't you worry about her, Chance."

The gambler watched his paddlewheeler steam upstream, disappearing behind a meandering turn in the wide river. As much as he wished to be aboard his own boat, he couldn't, not while Michael Balinger was still a free man.

"You did the right thing, Chance." This from Detective Jean Defoe, who approached the gambler and reached up to squeeze his shoulder in comfort. "We moved too fast for Balinger. He could not have foreseen your ability to secret Miss Walsh away to safety in so short a space of time.''

"I hope you're right. Until now Balinger's been running ten steps ahead of us.'' Chance turned to the smaller man. "What do we do now?''

Defoe pointed to a paddy wagon that waited at the end of the long wharf. "I've five men inside; I'm going back to the Walsh estate and search every inch of the plantation and then the bayou. If that doesn't dig up anything, I plan to stake out Alita's home tonight in case Kalitisca decides to visit her again.''

"Care for some company?'' Chance asked.

"Would you prefer to ride in your taxi or find a space in the paddy wagon?''

"I'll stick with Homer and Bad Bad,'' Chance answered with a wry smile on his lips. "There's something about police paddy wagons that makes me nervous.''

The detective grinned. "Understandable. Shall we be going?''

As the policeman hastened toward the paddy wagon, the gambler once more looked to the Mississippi. He had placed Anne aboard the *Wild Card* two hours after Elouise had died beneath the hooves of a wild mare. He could only hope that he had acted quickly enough to save the young woman's life.

"Gentlemen!'' Michael Balinger stood on the front steps of the Walsh mansion when Chance and Defoe pulled up in their separate vehicles. "I wondered where you had gone off to.''

The man extracted one of those new cigarettes from his coat pocket and lit it while the detective and gambler walked toward him. He exhaled a small cloud of smoke, watching the breeze dissipate it.

"Balinger, what are you doing here?" Defoe demanded.

Taking another drag from the cigarette, Balinger smiled. "I am still a neighbor to the Walshes. I was just paying them a neighborly visit to see how they were standing up during such difficult times."

The man paused, his smile spreading to a self-satisfied grin. "As it is, I understand only one of them is still standing. Graham's and Elouise's sudden deaths came as quite a surprise to me."

"Especially Elouise's," Chance said, his steel blue eyes narrowing as he studied the former sea captain.

"Especially hers." Balinger chuckled with obvious delight. "But then there are always little twists of fate none of us foresees."

"We know that you used the maid Alita to poison Graham and Rachael Walsh," Defoe said. "Also that you employed your Indian Kalitisca to kidnap her child and beat her into submission."

Balinger chuckled again. "Be careful, little man. You are treading on dangerous ground. Unless you have proof of those accusations, I believe a court of law would rule them slander."

"I'll have my proof." The detective stiffened, but did not back down from the man. "It's only a matter of time, Balinger. You've slipped up somewhere, and when I find where, you'll be swinging from the end of a rope."

"I don't think that's the way things will work out, my dear detective." Balinger dropped the butt of his cigarette to the ground and crushed it underfoot. "If the Walsh curse runs its course, this plantation will be mine in a matter of days. After all, only Anne survives her father—Anne and me.''

"You can forget Anne, Balinger," Chance spoke up. "I've made certain that she's in a place you'll never find her. She's safe from you now."

For an instant Balinger's expression darkened, and doubt dimmed the glinting light of his jet eyes, but just for an instant. His tone was a taunt when he answered the gambler. "Safe from *me?* I have no want of Anne Walsh. But a curse is a curse, Mr. Sharpe. How does one go about stopping the dark powers of the supernatural?"

With that, Balinger walked to a horse tied to a hitching post outside the mansion. He mounted and glanced back at the two men. "Good day, gentlemen."

"I wouldn't be grinning if I were you, Balinger," Chance called when the man nudged his horse toward the bayou. "The curse was on Graham Walsh and all his descendants—that includes bastard sons!"

Balinger's laughter rang out as he disappeared into the woods that fringed the bayou.

"Son of a bitch!" The first curse that Chance had ever heard Defoe utter spat from the small man's lips. "He goes too far! He pushes me beyond the limits of my endurance. He must be shown that he is not above the law!"

Chance merely looked at the detective. He agreed, but at the moment Balinger had covered his tracks too well.

"Come, we are going after the blackhearted whoreson." Defoe started toward the bayou. "I will greatly enjoy snapping handcuffs around his wrists and locking him behind bars."

Chance hurried to catch up with the detective as he entered the trees. "But I thought you said that there wasn't enough evidence against Balinger—that a high-powered attorney would have him on the street in a matter of minutes?"

"I did, and that's what will occur," Defoe replied while his short legs pumped at a furious pace. "But that makes no difference to me anymore. Hauling Balinger to the station house will be an inconvenience to him. It will waste his time and money. It will spoil his plans for the evening. Most of all, it will give me a modicum of satisfaction."

Chance smiled. He was beginning to like the way the detective thought. And pulling Balinger into a jail and slamming the bars behind him, if only for a few minutes, might, just might, shake the man up enough for him to make a mistake.

Neither policeman nor gambler spoke as the two men covered the two miles along the bayou path to Balinger's small farm. Defoe reached the door to the white house half a step ahead of Chance and rapped on the wood. When there was no answer, the detective didn't try again. He reached down, threw open the latch, and boldly strode inside. Chance nearly ran up the man's spine when Defoe halted without warning.

"What is this?" The detective's head snapped from side to side.

As did the gambler's! The house's parlor was empty—totally empty. The rest of Balinger's rooms were the same, including his weapon-laden study.

"He's gone." Defoe finally gave voice to the obvious. "My God, man, he's making a run for it!"

"Kalitisca!" Chance's mind raced. "If he's decided New Orleans is too hot for him, he'll go after the Indian!"

Defoe didn't answer, but ran from the house with the gambler at his heels.

* * *

Chance struck a match and held it over his head as he entered Kalitisca's shack. The flickering yellow glow revealed the same thing he had seen in Balinger's home—nothing!

"Everything's gone," Defoe said, disgust twisting his features. "The Indian has run off with Balinger."

Chance didn't argue. The shelves that had been lined with dusty bottles and vials now lay bare except for circles in the dust that marked where they had once stood.

"I moved too slowly," Defoe muttered to himself. "I should have realized Balinger might try something like this."

"Don't blame yourself," the gambler said. "Balinger didn't give any indication that he was about to run. Besides, if he took Kalitisca with him, that means the thread that connects Balinger to the Walsh murders is still intact. If we can find the Indian, we have Balinger right where we want him."

"If we can locate the Indian," Defoe replied. "And that, my friend, is a big if."

Chance walked into the police station and received directions to Detective Defoe's office from a cigar-chewing sergeant who looked as if he had sat in the same position for at least thirty years and had grown bored with that position twenty-nine years ago.

"Chance!" Defoe glanced up from a newspaper he read when the gambler entered his office. "I'm surprised to see you today. I understood that we were meeting for lunch tomorrow."

"We are," Chance replied, "but I thought that you might like to see this."

The gambler handed the smaller man a yellow sheet of paper. Defoe hastily scanned the single line it contained. He grinned up at Chance. "At least you have had some good news. Your friend Mr. Haver has successfully hidden Miss Walsh away in Independence, Missouri.''

"Independence was Jason's idea," Chance said. "If Balinger somehow traces her as far as Saint Louis, I doubt that he'll think of looking for her in Independence."

"I wish that I could also offer good news, but I can't. That Indian sighted in Baton Rouge turned out to be a Cherokee traveling with a medicine show," Defoe said as he handed the telegram back to the gambler.

"What do we do now?" Chance asked.

"We wait, my friend," the detective replied in a weary tone. "We wait, and we pray that we find Balinger before he finds Miss Walsh."

TWENTY-ONE

Chance slapped astringent onto his face, then slipped into a vest and coat. Walking to a window of his Hotel Burgundy suite, he drew back the curtains and threw open the window. A smile touched his lips as he sucked in a deep breath of the spring air.

Spring in the early morning hours only, he reminded himself. This was New Orleans. The heat and humidity would turn the day into a steam bath rivaling the summer in most American cities by mid-afternoon.

Long before that, Anne Walsh would be back in the city—the real reason for Chance's smile. She was due to arrive in three hours aboard the riverboat *Terlingua.* Two months had passed since he had secreted her from the city and placed the young woman in the care of his friend Jason Haver. During those two months, Michael Balinger had never been heard of nor seen. Only with Jean Defoe's assurance that the police would protect Anne had Chance suggested that she could return if she so wanted.

A knock came from the front door of the suite. The gambler turned from the window, walked from the bedroom, and opened the door. Homer A. Lincoln stood outside. He clutched a gray derby sporting a white rose tightly in his hands. The ivory grin that Chance associated with the cabbie was missing from the man's dark face.

"Homer, is there something wrong?"

"I don't know, Mr. Chance, but I reckoned that I should let you be the one to decide that for yourself." Homer's strained expression remained on his face. "The man done let Tye Watson off for good behavior. He's back in town, and he's lookin' for the Mojo Man."

Chance lifted a questioning eyebrow. "I don't see your point. I'm not looking for this Tye Watson."

"I know," Homer replied. "But you are lookin' to see the Mojo Man. Rumor is that he was seen last night back at his shack. If Tye gets to him 'fore you do, there won't be nothin' left of that Indian except small bloody pieces 'bout the size of ribbons."

"Kalitisca's been seen in New Orleans?" The gambler's eyes widened with interest. "Are you certain?"

"Three of my friends saw him at different times last night, Mr. Chance. For me that's as good as lookin' at him with my own eyeballs," the cabbie answered. "Better, in fact, 'cause I ain't got no want to lay my eyes on that devil man."

Chance snatched his wide-brimmed black hat from a wall peg and pulled it atop his head. "Homer, I have to see Detective Defoe as fast as possible!"

"I just was informed of the same rumors," the detective said after Chance repeated all that Homer had told him. "In fact, I was about to ride out to Kalitisca's shack. Would you care to accompany me?"

"Homer's waiting outside." Chance hurried the man from the office. "He'll get us there faster than any police paddy wagon."

The instant the two men settled into the cushions of his hack, Homer clucked Bad Bad to life and soon had the dappled gray mare moving through New Orleans's streets at a healthy clip. Chance stared out a window, watching the fashionable areas of the city give way to less reputable districts and finally to land that was more country than it was city. From his driver's board, Homer tugged on the reins and called out, "Whoa, Bad Bad."

The hack drew to a halt outside the run-down shack in which Kalitisca lived. Defoe slipped a hand behind his back and freed a blue-steel .32-caliber revolver. Chance pulled his belly-gun and cocked its hammer. With a nod from the detective, he opened the door and ran to the shack's door. There he and Defoe pressed an ear to the weathered boards, listening. No sound came from inside.

Without a word, Defoe reached down and flipped a wooden latch. His right foot lashed open, kicking the door inward. He then darted over the threshold with revolver raised and ready.

There was no need for the firearms: the Indian was nowhere to be seen. However, crate upon crate was packed into the tiny shack.

"They're Balinger's." Chance pointed to the name stenciled prominently on each of the wooden containers. "Have you heard that he's returned to New Orleans?"

The police detective shook his head. "But if Kalitisca is in town, I would wager that Balinger isn't far behind. Why else would his possessions be here?"

Defoe slowly examined the stacked crates, finally motioning for the gambler to join him. "No doubt that these belong to Balinger."

He tilted his head toward a crate that had been opened. Several of the pistols and rifles that had been packed inside lay atop the crates around them.

"It's as though someone dug through this crate for a specific weapon," Defoe said. "The Indian? Or perhaps Balinger?"

Chance didn't want to hazard a guess. The cold chill that flowed up his spine couldn't be ignored. If either Kalitisca or Balinger had wanted a weapon, there could be but one reason. "Anne! The son of a bitch is going after Anne!"

"My God!" Defoe pivoted and stared at the gambler. "She's due back in the city today, isn't she?"

"In exactly one hour," Chance answered as he read the face of his pocket watch. "I'm supposed to meet her at the wharf."

"We'll both meet her." The detective grabbed the gambler's elbow and shoved him toward the door. "My fear is that another also has plans to greet her."

The *Terlingua*'s steam whistle screamed its arrival in New Orleans. However, Chance's eyes weren't on the riverboat. He scanned the crowd that gathered on the wharf to meet the paddlewheeler, searching for Michael Balinger or his Indian henchman.

"We have the pier covered, my friend," Defoe said from beside the gambler. "The ten officers I strung around the wharf will not let either of them through."

Chance nodded, but lacked the confidence in New Orleans's finest that the detective displayed. On more than one occasion he had easily evaded police who raided the French Quarter's gambling dens. If he could do that, he held no doubts that Balinger could do the same if necessary.

"There she is."

Defoe's pointing finger drew Chance's gaze to the *Terlingua*'s boiler deck. Wearing a dress of bright yellow, Anne stood at the rail waving to the gambler. Chance felt his pulse double its tempo when he raised an arm and returned the wave. In their months apart he had forgotten how beautiful the delicate woman was.

Motioning for a steward to lift her bags, Anne moved with the crowd down the stairway that led to the steamer's main deck. As she stepped onto the gangplank, a shot rang out!

Horror turned the gambler's blood to ice when he saw Anne's body stiffen. A blossom of crimson flowered on the breast of her bright yellow dress. Her gold-flecked eyes stared at Chance, filled with bewilderment, as though she was unable to comprehend what had happened to her. In the next moment, her legs gave way and she collapsed to the gangplank.

Ignoring the terrified screams that rose from the women on the pier and paddlewheeler, Chance shoved his way through the crowd, kneeling beside Anne's crumpled form.

"Anne? Anne?" He lifted her head and cradled it in his lap. "Anne, answer me."

No endearing whisper came from her still lips; no word of love or caring would ever pass from those lips again.

"Nooooo!" Chance groaned as he hugged Anne's lifeless body to his breast. "Noooo."

"Detective Defoe." A blue-uniformed policeman elbowed a path to the officer who stood above the gambler. "We've sighted him. A blond sailor atop that warehouse did the shooting. Five of our men saw him leap from the roof. They're giving chase."

"Chance"—Defoe looked down at the gambler— "I'm going after him. He's our lead to Balinger, I'm certain of it."

While the detective and the other officer moved back through the crowd, Chance gently placed Anne's head on the ground. "He'll pay for what he's done to you. I promise you that."

Pushing to his feet, the gambler chased after the two policemen. Following the pointing arms of two other officers, they moved down an alley that ran between two warehouses. Exiting the alley, they found another officer rubbing a sprained ankle; he urged them down a wide avenue and into yet another alley. There they found four policemen standing beside a garbage bin.

"What is it?" Defoe demanded when he reached the men.

"These," one of the policemen said, holding up a red striped shirt and a pair of blue trousers. "He was wearing these."

"And apparently this," another officer added, displaying a blond theatrical wig that he had found atop the discarded clothing.

"Balinger!" The name came from the gambler's lips like a curse.

Realizing that the man had worn a disguise to kill the sole remaining obstacle between him and the Walsh fortune, the gambler pushed past the police and sprinted to the end of the alley, hoping to glimpse the escaping killer. What he found was a busy thoroughfare filled with carriages and hacks. Balinger was nowhere in sight.

"Damn! The bastard did it, and he got away!" The gambler could not contain his seething anger and frustration. "How, dammit? How in hell did he do it?"

"He was ready for us, Chance. That's how." Defoe walked to the gambler. "Come, there's nothing more that we can do here."

"But there is something we can do at Kalitisca's shack. Sooner or later, either Balinger or the Indian has to show up. And when they do, they'll find me waiting for them!"

Without waiting for the detective to reply, Chance spun around and stalked from the alley. He had a debt that he intended to settle, and would stand for no interference until the task was done.

TWENTY-TWO

Chance resisted the urge to light the slender, black saber cigar. The flare of a match or even the cherry glow of burning tobacco was too risky. In spite of their location—crouched behind the bole of an ancient live oak a quarter of a mile down the road from Kalitisca's shack and the half-moon above—it was night, and any light might give them away. Instead, the gambler shifted the cigar from one side of his mouth to the other and chewed at its end.

Detective Jean Defoe half turned his head and glanced at his companion. The moon's frosty light washed across his features that were twisted with disdain as though to reprimand the gambler for a disgusting habit.

Chance ignored the policeman and spat to one side—in a thin stream of brown spittle—the tobacco juices that filled his mouth. After occupying the same small portion of real estate since the late hours of morning, going without either food or water, he refused to be denied the simple pleasure of tobacco, even if he had to chew it.

The jingle and clank of distant chains drew the gambler's mind from the detective. He scanned the dirt road to the east. A horse and wagon appeared like phantoms in the moon's glow.

"Another road wagon." Defoe nudged Chance's side and handed him a pair of binoculars.

Lifting the field glasses to his eyes, the gambler focused on the slowly lumbering vehicle. The detective was right. It was yet another road wagon with an empty flat bed. The road wagon traffic on the rutted road surprised Chance. This was at least the tenth such wagon that had passed by since late evening.

Before returning the binoculars to Defoe, Chance surveyed the road for as far as he could see. Still no sign of either Balinger or of his Indian henchman.

The gambler shoved the doubts that crowded into his head away, refusing to examine them. He couldn't delve their logic—not without breaking down and perhaps losing his sanity. Balinger or Kalitisca had to show up—had to!

For the thousandth time since beginning the stakeout with Defoe, Chance's mind waded through that morning's events. He relived the terrible moment when a single rifle bullet slammed into Anne's fragile body, leaving her dead on the *Terlingua*'s gangplank. He chased the fleeing murderer through the alleys and streets only to discover that he had once again eluded pursuit.

The details of exactly how Balinger had learned of Anne's return to New Orleans might never be known, Chance realized. But he could think of a thousand ways to learn the names of the passengers traveling the Mississippi River.

It shouldn't have taken too much for Balinger to put two and two together and come up with the fact that Chance had secreted Anne away on the *Wild Card.* Nor that St. Louis would be her logical destination. That much aside, it was merely a matter of greasing the palms of enough booking agents to guarantee that he was notified the moment that Anne Walsh purchased a ticket heading downriver.

He had to strike the final blow in New Orleans, Chance silently reflected. Balinger's ego demanded that. He had to kill the sole surviving Walsh right under their noses and get away with it to prove once and for all his superiority to the imperfect humans who surrounded him.

It seemed so clear and obvious now, with the gift of hindsight. Why hadn't Defoe, "a trained and experienced sleuth," seen it before? Why hadn't the police . . .

Chance caught himself. Nothing was to be gained by blaming Anne's death on Defoe and the police. It was too easy to believe others shouldered all the fault. The truth was, he was partly to blame. He understood Balinger as much as the detective, had seen the man's insidious genius do its deadly work. And he was the seasoned river traveler and owner of a paddlewheeler. He should have realized how easy it was to keep tabs on steamer passengers. But he hadn't, no more than had the police.

We grew complacent. He recognized that time had dulled his wits. For two months Balinger and Kalitisca had disappeared. There was a seed of truth in the hackneyed old saying "Out of sight, out of mind." Without Balinger's constant presence, the man's danger seemed somehow distant and less real and malignant. He was certain that Balinger had realized this and had taken full advantage of that weakness in human nature. Men like Balinger fed and fattened on the weaknesses of others.

Now the man stood so very close to achieving his murderous goal. He all but had his hands on the wealth that once had belonged to Graham Walsh. There was but a single untidy thread of evidence that connected

Balinger to six calculated, cold-blooded murders—Kalitisca. Without the Indian—if he was still alive and not already butchered by the former sea captain—Balinger would inherit a fortune without a shadow of the horrors he had committed ever touching him.

Oh, murders had been committed, all right. No one could doubt that Graham and Rachael Walsh and their daughter Anne had been murdered. But unless Kalitisca was arrested and broken down into testifying against Balinger, the maid Alita would hang for Graham's and Rachael's murders, and Anne's killing would be eventually filed away among the unsolved cases. All the while, Balinger would be laughing inside the house that once had belonged to a father who had never given him his name.

"Chance . . ." Defoe nudged the gambler's side again. "Something or someone is moving out there behind the shack."

The gambler accepted the binoculars and focused them. His pulse raced. That someone was Kalitisca! He was certain of it, even in the dim light. The Indian crept to the back of the shack, glanced cautiously around him, then darted through the front door.

"It's Kalitisca." Chance pointed to a yellow glow that illuminated the shack's only front window as a light was lit inside. "Let's go get him."

Defoe nodded, slipping his revolver from a holster hung at the back of his belt. "But go slow and easy— and please keep low! We don't want him to see us until it's too late for him to make a break."

Chance nodded as he pulled out a .44-caliber Remington and nestled it in his right hand.

"And, Chance, remember," the detective added, "you're to cover the back window, and I go in through the front."

Again the gambler nodded his acceptance. It was the plan they had agreed upon hours earlier. Although Chance noted a touch of apprehension in Defoe's eyes, the gambler held no such doubts. He had no intention of suddenly taking justice into his own hands. The Indian would not die tonight, not if he could help it. Without Kalitisca, there was no way to get at Balinger, and he was the man Chance wanted.

In a low crouch—the overgrown weeds and grass in the empty field between them and the shack concealing their movements—the two men edged forward. Chance sucked in a series of deep breaths to still the runaway race of his pounding heart. This was it—the slipup that both he and Defoe had prayed for since they had realized that Balinger was behind the Walsh murders. The man was not perfect; he made mistakes, although not many. And this mistake was going to cost him his life!

Halfway to the shack, the detective held out an arm to halt the gambler. He then pointed to the approaching road wagon. "We'll wait until it passes. If the Indian is nervous, the sound of its approach will have him at the window to make sure that it's not the police. We can't risk him glimpsing us."

Chance silently agreed as he settled back on his heels to wait for the wagon to roll by. Kalitisca was too big a fish to let him slip off the hook at this point because of a stupid mistake.

The jangle of the road wagon's heavy chains grew louder as the two-horse team pulled their ponderous burden over the rutted dirt road. The driver looked to be more asleep than awake. His shoulders slumped forward and his head hung low, lolling from side to side with each jostling bump of the wheels. Chance didn't blame him for his lack of attentiveness to his team. The hour grew late, and most men had long ago retired to the comfort of their beds.

"Patience, my friend," Defoe whispered, as though expecting the gambler to suddenly bolt toward the shack. "In a few more minutes the Indian will be ours."

Chance only half listened to the detective. His eyes narrowed, and he exhaled his breath in a soft whistle through clenched teeth.

Ten feet from the front of the shack, the wagon's driver awoke. His head turned from side to side, searching the area around him. Then he abruptly stood and scanned the night on all four sides. The moon's silvery light struck his face like the beam of a spotlight.

Balinger! Chance reached out and shoved Defoe facedown in the grass, then threw himself forward, unwilling to risk detection this late in the game.

"My God," Defoe whispered when he rose just enough to peek above the top of the high grass. "What fortunate luck! Our Captain Balinger has grown sloppy."

Tugging on the reins, Balinger drew the two-horse team to a halt directly in front of the shack. He cautiously surveyed the night once more before tying the horses, then leaping from the wagon. In the batting of an eye, he rushed inside the Indian's shack.

Chance remembered Defoe's comment of months ago that Balinger would not get rid of Kalitisca until the man no longer had a use for the Indian. It was now apparent that Balinger had at least one last task for his henchman before he disposed of Kalitisca. The Indian was to help him load the crates in the shack onto the road wagon. His possessions secured, Balinger would sever that one slender thread tying him to the Walsh murders and ride away a free and rich man.

Defoe pushed back into a crouch and motioned the gambler forward with a wave of his hand. Using the wagon that Balinger had left outside the shack as cover, they hastened forward, stopping only when they pressed against the side of the road wagon.

"I still want you to cover the back," Defoe whispered. "We'll handle it just as we planned. And remember, I want no shooting unless absolutely necessary. Balinger and the Indian are going to be brought to justice for their crimes."

Chance tilted his head and edged toward the back of the wagon. "Give me two minutes to get into position."

"Two minutes," Defoe repeated.

Chance took a step out from the wagon's cover and immediately jerked back. Someone approached the shack from the rear. He motioned Defoe to his side and nodded to the black-skinned man who crept through the tall grass.

Although the gambler had never laid eyes on the muscular black man before, he knew him instantly— Tye Watson! Recently released from prison, the man had returned to find Kalitisca just as Homer had predicted he would.

Before either Chance or Defoe could react, the massive black man shot to the shack's front door, threw it open, and rushed in.

"What the hell!" Balinger's shocked voice railed from inside. "Who is this?"

"I come to repay you for what you done to my Callie, you foreign heathen," boomed a deep male voice that Chance had never heard.

"Come closer, black man, and I'll show you exactly what I did to your precious wife after I grew tired of her," challenged a third voice that the gambler recognized as the same voice that had come from the ghostly apparition at the Walshes' dinner party two months ago.

"Kalitisca, get him out of here," Balinger demanded. "We haven't time for your petty disputes."

Defoe tapped Chance on the shoulder. "Come on, we've got to get in there before the fireworks begin. I don't want to lose Balinger and the Indian."

Chance didn't argue. At the detective's side he started for the shack's open door.

"I'll cut your—"

Kalitisca's voice broke an instant before the blast of a shotgun unloading both barrels rent the night like thunder.

"No!" Defoe shouted, sprinting for the door. "No, dammit, no!"

And was nearly knocked off his feet by a fleeing Tye Watson, who ran from the shack with eyes round in fear and sweat beading his face.

For a moment Defoe paused as though considering whether to chase Watson or proceed on his original course. The shack won out. He hastened through the door, pistol level and ready.

From over the detective's shoulder, Chance took in the interior scene in one hasty glance. Michael Balinger stood pressed against the far wall paralyzed in fear. Blood splattered the front of the workman's clothes he wore. His saucer-wide eyes were locked to the twisted body of a half-naked Indian who lay on the floor. A few feet away from Kalitisca's body lay a gold-and-silver inlaid shotgun from Balinger's collection. It was one of the weapons Chance had seen earlier that day, when he and Defoe discovered the open crate—the same crate from which Balinger had selected the rifle used to kill Anne, of that the gambler was certain.

Kalitisca, Chance thought as his gut tightened—or what was left of him. What had once been his stomach and half his chest was now no more than a crimson-oozing mass of flesh turned to jelly—testimony to the destructive force of the buckshot that Tye Watson had fired into the Indian's body at point-blank range.

The instant Chance's mind reconstructed the scenario of death that had transpired within the shack in the passage of a few seconds, he recognized the consequences. With Kalitisca's death, they had lost the one man who could identify Balinger as the real force behind the Walsh curse, the man who had masterminded the eradication of a whole family so that he might inherit Graham Walsh's fortune.

By a grotesque twist of fate, Balinger had won. He had murdered six innocent people and gotten away with it. There would be no gallows for Graham Walsh's bastard son.

Chance glanced at Defoe. The small detective's expression said that the man had reached the same conclusion—Balinger had escaped them in spite of all their efforts. Defoe's eyes slowly lifted to Balinger.

"Detective!" The fear that had gripped Balinger's face faded the instant that his own gaze fell upon Defoe. "My God, man, don't just stand there. Go after him. He'll get away!"

"Him?" Defoe questioned. "Who are you talking about, Balinger?"

"The black man who ran out of here just as you were coming in," Balinger answered with urgency. "He shot Kalitisca. You can't let him get away!"

"Raise your hands over your head, Balinger, and don't try anything stupid. I'd enjoy having to put a bullet between your eyes, I really would," Defoe said, his voice cold and hard, leaving no doubt that he wasn't lying.

"Raise my hands? What are you talking about, man?" A hint of doubt and panic tightened Balinger's tone. His eyes darted about the room. "Aren't you going after that man?"

"Balinger, I'm placing you under arrest for the murder of your former manservant, the Indian Kalitisca," Defoe replied, his pistol leveled directly at Balinger's head. "Formal charges will be filed as soon as I've booked you down at the station."

Chance's head jerked around, uncertain that he had heard the detective correctly. Defoe's expression was set like granite.

"Arresting me?" Balinger's voice went up an octave. "But I didn't do anything!"

"That shotgun belongs to you, doesn't it?" The detective tilted his head to the weapon on the floor.

"Yes, it's mine. But I didn't fire it. I . . ."

Defoe cut him off. "Your weapon and your clothes are soaked with the blood of your victim. On top of that, I arrived at the scene less than a second or two after I heard the shotgun go off. There's not a judge or a jury in Louisiana who won't convict you, Balinger."

A humorless smile spread over Chance's lips as he saw what Defoe had in mind. Legally it was wrong, dead wrong. But he and the detective had come here tonight to serve justice—and it *would* be served.

"No," Balinger's head moved from side to side in denial. "You know I didn't do it. You saw the man who ran out that door."

"No one ran from the door," Defoe said. "I've been watching this shack since noon, and the only people to enter here have been you and the Indian. You killed him, Balinger, the evidence is clear, and you'll hang for it."

"But you had to see—" Balinger looked like a trapped animal as the realization of the situation penetrated his brain. His eyes shot to Chance. "You had to see the other man, Sharpe. You couldn't have missed him. He ran you over as you came through the door."

The gambler met Balinger's pleading gaze, and with ice in his voice answered, "There was no one else, Baligner, only you and Kalitisca. There's no way you can escape this murder."

"No! Damn the both of you! There's no way you can get away with this! My attorney will—"

Defoe's right arm snaked out, slamming the pistol he held into the side of Balinger's head. The man groaned, his eyes rolled, and he collapsed to the shack's floor unconscious.

"Criminals are all the same," Defoe said while he pulled a pair of handcuffs from a pocket and snapped them around Balinger's wrists. "They're never guilty even when they're caught red-handed."

The detective stood and faced his companion. "You realize that you'll be called on to testify at the trial, don't you, Chance? Can you handle that?"

Chance nodded without hesitation. "Only Balinger and Kalitisca were in this shack."

"Good," Defoe answered with a smile of relief. "I want you to tell that to a prosecutor; then I think it would be best if you made yourself scarce around New Orleans until the trial. The less opportunity Balinger's lawyers have to talk with you, the better."

"No problem," Chance said. "No problem at all."

TWENTY-THREE

"Whoa, Bad Bad." Homer drew the taxi to a halt and bent down to peer at the single passenger in the hack. "Mr. Chance, if'n you don't mind, this is as close as I'm goin'. I ain't got no want to see what's fixin' to happen. I can read 'bout it in the mornin' papers."

The gambler nodded when he stepped from the cab. "I understand, Homer. But I would appreciate if you would wait here for me. I shouldn't be gone that long."

"I'll be right here," the cabbie assured him.

Chance turned from the taxi and walked down a narrow side street toward an open square. In truth, he would rather read about this in a newspaper than actually witness it—a hanging was not a pretty thing to see. However, he *had* to see this one. He owed that much to Anne and the other members of her family who had died at Balinger's hand.

Reaching the end of the street, he stared across the square to the wooden gallows constructed at its center. A single rope swayed slightly in the morning breeze. Two official-appearing men stood by a wooden lever. The hangman and a priest, Chance realized.

Although morbid curiosity moved the onlookers inward to form a tight circle around the gallows, the gambler hung back. He had no desire to be any closer.

"It'll be over in a few minutes," the voice of Detective Jean Defoe intruded the gambler's thoughts. "The guard is bringing him from the prison now." Defoe paused and studied the taller man's face. "Has time brought any regrets, Chance?"

"No." Chance shook his head. "I'd still handle it the way we did. Although I'd prefer that he had been tried for his real crimes."

"Justice is blind," was all Defoe replied.

Chance looked back to the gallows. Four guards now led Michael Balinger into the square from another side street. The man looked small, with his head hung chin on chest as the crowd jeered his passage. Slowly the guards helped him up the ten stairs that led to the waiting noose.

The gambler drew a deep breath to steady himself for what would soon come. He could not escape the irony of the situation. Balinger had killed six innocent people and the law couldn't touch him. Yet, in a few more minutes he would die for a murder he hadn't committed. Justice *was* blind. In part, Balinger would hang because Chance had perjured himself on the witness stand, denying repeatedly that he had never seen another man enter Kalitisca's shack the night the Indian had been killed.

High on the gallows, one of the guards read from a paper he unfolded, repeating Balinger's crimes and ordering that the sentence of death by hanging be carried out. While two of the guards held the man's arms, another slipped a black hood over his head, then dropped the noose around his neck and tightened it. The priest chanted in Latin, praying for Balinger's eternal soul. While the prayer droned on, the hangman clutched the lever with both hands and wrenched back hard.

The trapdoor dropped out from under Balinger's boots. He fell six feet before the play in the rope ended. The man's body jerked violently, and the harsh sound of his breaking neck echoed across the square. Then it was over except for the reflexive jerking and spasmodic twisting of his body as the last sparks of life fled the muscles of his arms and legs.

"Justice has been served," Defoe said softly. "Perhaps not the way we would have preferred, but served just the same."

Chance said nothing; he simply turned and started back to the waiting taxi. Defoe trotted after him. "You look pale, my friend. Would you like to go somewhere for a drink to fortify yourself?"

The gambler stopped abruptly and faced the detective. "Defoe, I've been a man whose creed has always been fair play at the gaming tables and in life. When those I know are cheated, I'm willing to do anything to right their wrongs—short of murder. I know that what we did was right, but I can't stop feeling that I crossed that line today, breaking my own creed. I feel dirty, and it's not the kind of dirt a man can wash away with soap and hot water. I hope you understand when I say that I don't want to see you or New Orleans for a long time. I have to return to the river and try to forget about Balinger, what he did, and what we had to do to him."

Without giving the policeman a chance to answer, the gambler pivoted and walked to the cab. He called up to Homer to drive him to the wharves. There the *Wild Card* waited to take him upriver, away from the filth of the city.

The Maverick with the Winning Hand

A blazing new series of Western excitement featuring a high-rolling rogue with a thirst for action!

by Clay Tanner

CHANCE 75160-7/$2.50US/$3.50Can
Introducing Chance—a cool-headed, hot-blooded winner.

CHANCE #2 75161-5/$2.50US/$3.50Can
Riverboat Rampage

CHANCE #3 75162-3/$2.50US/$3.50Can
Dead Man's Hand

CHANCE #4 75163-1/$2.50US/$3.50Can
Gambler's Revenge

CHANCE #5 75164-X/$2.50US/$3.50Can
Delta Raiders

CHANCE #6 75165-8/$2.50US/$3.50Can
Mississippi Rogue

CHANCE #7 75390-1/$2.50US/$3.50Can
Dakota Showdown